PENGUIN BOOKS
GENTLY FALLS THE BAKULA

Sudha Murty was born in 1950 in Shiggaon in north Karnataka. She did her M.Tech. in Computer Science, and is now the chairperson of the Infosys Foundation. A prolific writer in English and Kannada, she has written nine novels, four technical books, three travelogues, one collection of short stories, three collections of non-fiction pieces and two books for children.

Her books have been translated into all the major Indian languages and have sold over 300,000 copies around the country. She was the recipient of the R.K. Narayan's Award for Literature and the Padma Shri in 2006.

Other books by Sudha Murty

Fiction
The Magic Drum and Other Stories (Puffin)
Mahashweta
Dollar Bahu

Non-fiction
Wise and Otherwise
The Old Man and His God
How I Taught My Grandmother to Read
and Other Stories (Puffin)

Gently Falls the Bakula

SUDHA MURTY

PENGUIN BOOKS

PENGUIN BOOKS

Published by the Penguin Group

Penguin Books India Pvt. Ltd, 11 Community Centre, Panchsheel Park,
New Delhi 110 017, India

Penguin Group (USA) Inc., 375 Hudson Street, New York, New York 10014,
USA

Penguin Group (Canada), 90 Eglinton Avenue East, Suite 700, Toronto, Ontario,
M4P 2Y3, Canada (a division of Pearson Penguin Canada Inc.)

Penguin Books Ltd, 80 Strand, London WC2R 0RL, England

Penguin Ireland, 25 St Stephen's Green, Dublin 2, Ireland (a division of Penguin
Books Ltd)

Penguin Group (Australia), 707 Collins Street, Melbourne, Victoria 3008, Australia
(a division of Pearson Australia Group Pty Ltd)

Penguin Group (NZ), 67 Apollo Drive, Rosedale, Auckland 0632,
New Zealand (a division of Pearson New Zealand Ltd)

Penguin Group (South Africa) (Pty) Ltd, Block D, Rosebank Office Park,
181 Jan Smuts Avenue, Parktown North, Johannesburg 2193, South Africa

Penguin Books Ltd, Registered Offices: 80 Strand, London WC2R 0RL, England

First published by Penguin Books India 2008
Copyright © Sudha Murty 2008

Typeset in Sabon by S.R. Enterprises, New Delhi
Printed at Replika Press Pvt. Ltd, Sonepat

ALWAYS LEARNING **PEARSON**

To all those women who allowed family commitments and responsibilities to overpower their own aspirations

PREFACE

This was my first novel in Kannada, written about three decades back. It was extremely well received then.

I had not seen the corporate world from close and only imagined how it functioned. But now, in real life, I have seen it all. I am aware that industrialization, technological progress and scientific advancement are necessary and bring prosperity to our country, but they have their own shortcomings. They create a whole set of problems, sociological and psychological.

This novel is set in north Karnataka in the 1980s, so it may appear outdated in some parts. But the story is such that it can happen in any part of the country, even today. There must be innumerable couples who have been through, and are still going through, such dilemmas, be it in a small town or a mega city.

I have chosen Hubli and Bombay as the setting for the novel. These two places are very dear to my heart, since I grew up in one place and in the other, I have enjoyed working.

I would like to thank Keerti Ramachandra for editing the manuscript and Penguin for publishing the novel.

Sudha Murty
Bangalore

It was a day of great excitement for the students of Model High School, Hubli. The results of the district-level interschool essay competition were to be announced that morning. The competition, open to students of the tenth standard, was a prestigious one not because of the prize money, but because the award had been instituted by a highly respected essayist. The prize-winning essay would be sent to the state-level competition.

The hall was abuzz with anticipation. The boys were in animated discussion, the girls in whispered speculation. Competitions such as these invariably threw up unexpected winners. Ugly ducklings often turn into beautiful swans when they are tested. So who was it going to be this time? The suspense was palpable.

When the history teacher Mr Kulkarni walked in, a sudden hush fell upon the room. Sensing the tension in the air, Mr Kulkarni decided to prolong the suspense a little longer.

He began by saying, 'I know all of you are waiting impatiently for the results of the essay competition and to know who the winner is. But I am going to ask you to wait a little longer. I will read out the essay first and allow you to guess who the author of it could be. After hearing the essay I am sure you will agree that it is a most mature and heartwarming effort, definitely deserving of the prize.'

A few ooohs and mild protests of 'tell us first, Sir,' were quickly silenced, as Mr Kulkarni began to read:

'All are my children . . .
I am like their father.
Like any father wishes for his child,
Happiness and comfort,
I wish that for all human beings;
Eternal joy.
Wherever I am,
Whether I am having my dinner or at a party,
Whether attending to matters of secrecy, or inspecting
the cattle pens,
Whether on a journey or resting in my garden,
Informers must bring me the news of my subjects.
Wherever I am I will work relentlessly to benefit my
people.
Sacred of all duties is the path of dharma.
A man who is not conscious cannot follow dharma.
Dharma should flourish; not perish
Let people strive for its growth,
And not wish its destruction!'

These are words inscribed on the stone edicts of
Devanampiya Piyadassi Ashoka. Ashoka, the son of
Bimbisara and grandson of Chandragupta Maurya has
earned for himself a special place in the history of the world.
There have been many great kings who fought wars and
won major battles—like Alexander. There were great
saints, full of compassion and who showed kindness to all
living creatures, like Christ and Buddha. But the combination
of a king and a saint there was none, other than Ashoka.

Emperor Ashoka was a great human being. After the
battle of Kalinga, he saw the terrible suffering inflicted on
the people as a result of the war and he was horrified. His
heart melted and he decided to be more tolerant and
compassionate and dedicated the rest of his life to the

practice and preaching of Dharma. He began to look upon his subjects as his children and did everything for their welfare.

When we study his rock edicts, we understand the nature of this noble king and come to know his valuable thoughts about Dharma.

Perhaps, Ashoka did not have a change of heart and turn to non-violence merely because of the Kalinga war! That event may have merely acted as a spur for an already gentle and sensitive emperor.

'Ashoka had his edicts etched throughout the kingdom, on pillars, on stones and in caves. It is said his kingdom stretched from Karnataka in the south to Pakistan and the borders of Afghanistan in the north; from the Arabian Sea in the west to what is now Orissa (then Kalinga) in the east. He had them inscribed in Pali, Prakrit, Brahmi and Aremic so that his message would reach the common man. He has described the Kalinga war too in some instances. It is said that in those days when the population was small, one hundred thousand people were killed in the war and the river Daya, on the banks of which the war was fought, had flowed red with blood. A hundred and fifty thousand people were taken away as prisoners. One can imagine the horrors of that war!

'Some of the edicts of the emperor can be found in Maski, Gavi Mata in Raichur district and Siddapura in Chitradurga district. That it was Ashoka who was known as Devanampiya and Piyadassi, the Maski stone edict was the first to reveal.

'The edicts inform us that he was a great warrior, kind to his subjects, a worthy emperor and a deeply religious ruler. Today the kingdom of Ashoka does not exist. But the principles of the five ideals known as *"Panchasheela"*, formulated by him, are the greatest treasures he has left to this modern world of conflicts. The systems of administration he set up are commendable! That is why the name of Ashoka, who did not remain merely "dear of gods" but also "dear of people", is today shining bright not only in the history of India but also in the history of the world. I salute such an emperor.

'India, which boasted of such a kind monarch, is blessed. It is a land as holy as he who ruled it. The ancient Kannada poet Pampa wrote:

This land is so pious and sacred, that
If I am not reborn as a human being in this land,
God, then please make me a singing cuckoo or a
humming bee at least!

'I too pray to god that I may be born again and again in such a country.'

By this time, though the name had not yet been announced, each one in the class knew that it could only be Ms Shrimati Deshpande who could have written such an essay.

Ms Shrimati Deshpande was a slim, tall girl, with a wheatish complexion and good, clear features. She had unusually long hair that reached below her knees. She always wore a string of bakula flowers in her hair. Shrimati was one of the brightest students in her class.

So when the teacher finally announced her name as the winner of the competition, her classmates were not surprised. They broke into loud applause. The shy Shrimati was happy but embarrassed. Luckily, the bell rang just then so the teacher quickly handed her the essay before all the students rushed out.

As Shrimati was gathering her books and getting ready to go home, she overheard the conversation of some boys

Sudha Murty

from her class. They were engrossed in a discussion about the best essay. They were expressing their surprise that Shrikant Deshpande had not got the first prize. Shrikant was Shrimati's rival in the class. A tall, fair and handsome young man, he was known for his strong determination to be the best. Now that he was beaten in this essay competition, his friends Mallesh Shetty and Ravi Patil were most upset, even more than Shrikant himself. It was a matter of prestige for them, and the thought that Shrimati had defeated him was hard to accept. They were venting their anger on Shrikant. This kind of rivalry was very common in the co-ed schools of those days.

'Shrikant, you shouldn't have given her a chance this time,' fumed Ravi Patil.

Shrikant smilingly replied, 'Take it easy, Ravi. History is not a great subject. Can just one good essay make you a topper? Writing an essay is nothing but filling up pages. Real intelligence is scoring in science.'

'Don't yap too much, Shrikant! All of us are aware that Shrimati is not a dumb girl. Accept your defeat with grace. She is intelligent and hardworking and will definitely score better than you in every subject if you don't look out,' retorted Ravi.

Mallesh was nodding his head in agreement. 'Come on, Mallya,' said Shrikant to his dear friend, 'you also don't overestimate her. I agree she is good but only in arts subjects like history and languages. Normally women are very fond of history because it is an accumulation of gossip—like some emperor had three wives, the last wife had six sons, etc. This doesn't require any logic or reasoning, only memorizing facts, which girls are good at.'

'How do you know?' Ravi questioned Shrikant.

'You know that I am her neighbour, Ravi. I can see her studying from my room. Every day she gets up at dawn, probably to prepare such kind of essays. If I had also prepared like her, I would have written a better one.' None of his friends were prepared to accept the excuses Shrikant was making for his failure.

'Don't fool us, Shrikant. Why would you wake up so early? Is it to just watch her studying? We know that you are also as hardworking as her but she is any day brighter than you. My mother was scolding me saying none of us do anything, except roam around, but Shrimati does all the housework and also studies. I think my mother is right.'

Mallesh was upset with Shrikant because he knew that he couldn't beat Shrimati and no words of Shrikant could console him.

As the boys started walking out, Ravi Patil said to Mallesh, 'Mallya, you are so thick-skinned! Why are you getting so upset when Shrikant is not? He is conceding defeat so easily. Why? Because when a person is in love, he is ready to accept defeat. Have you not noticed why Shrikant always gives away his first position to her? Because she is going to be his better half! See even their names match—*Shrimati-Shrikant Deshpande*. One day you will understand the finer feelings of love, Mallya, don't worry.' So saying Ravi burst out laughing.

Shrimati turned around, red with embarrassment, and saw Shrikant staring at her. He too looked baffled and felt equally idiotic.

After a moment or two, he exploded, 'Shut up you fools! Don't just speak whatever comes to your mouth. There is nothing like that! It's all your imagination. I was not responsible for her name. If you have the guts go and ask her.'

He was sure that they would not ask Shrimati!

In North Karnataka a married woman's name consisted of her first name, followed by her husband's name and then the surname. In the case of an unmarried girl, her father's name was her middle name.

Poor Shrimati! Her name, which was the name of Lakshmi, the goddess of wealth, was also a signifier for a married woman. And her father's name was Shrikant! Both she and Shrikant had the same surname—Deshpande.

This unusual combination of names had led to all the jokes and teasing that she had just heard. But neither Shrikant nor Shrimati could do anything to stop it.

Shrimati quickly walked out of the school with her classmates Vandana Patil and Sharada Emmikeri. She was in no mood to talk. An extremely sensitive person by nature, she had overheard all the comments that the boys had made and she was embarrassed. She and Shrikant had been classmates from the first standard and they had been neighbours for generations. But there was a bitter rivalry between the two families, from the times of their forefathers. They had once owned lands adjoining each other's and their enmity intruded into their homes even today.

Shrimati did not like the kind of loose talk the boys had indulged in and she wanted to talk about her discomfiture to someone. Since she had no sisters or brothers, she could only talk to her friends. But that day, even her friends were too excited about her winning the prize, and were in no mood to listen to anything.

'Shrimati, I am so glad that Shrikant was put down today. And with him his friends. That Mallesh Shetty, he talks such rubbish, making fun of us girls all the time. As for Ravi Patil, he thinks no end of himself! All said and done, the fact is our schoolmates have no manners. They don't know how to behave. You served them right.'

'Shrimati, I read a woman's brain weighs less than a man's. Is it true?' Sharada was a little worried.

'Shari,' Shrimati said affectionately, 'you should know that intelligence is independent of weight!'

'I was confused, Shrimati. I am not as bright as you are, see!' After a pause she continued, 'But you know that

Shrikant's mother Gangakka and his maternal uncle Sheenappa, they think that he is the brightest star in the sky. Sheenappa keeps coming to our shop and talks non-stop about his nephew. I had taken a vow with god Hanuman of Bhandiwad village that if you beat Shrikant in the final exam, I will distribute special pedas to everyone in school. These Deshpandes are too much. Even though they do not have any lands left, their arrogance has not diminished.'

Vandana Patil pinched Sharada's hand to stop her but Sharada was not so bright as to understand that this kind of comment would hurt Shrimati. After all she too was the daughter of a landless Deshpande!

Bhandiwad is a small village near Hubli and the local deity, Hanuman, is very famous for bestowing great boons upon his devotees. There is a strong belief that if someone requested a favour and fasted on Saturdays, their requests would be fulfilled. In return, they just had to offer some sweets to him to thank him for the boon. Since the pedas of Dharwad were very famous, so much so that people of North Karnataka said that if you hadn't eaten the peda your life was wasted, Sharada had promised to offer them, nothing less.

The other well-known temple in that region was the Railway Eshwar temple in Hubli, a busier, more populous, commercial town than Dharwad. The small Eshwar temple was adjacent to the railway station, so the presiding deity came to be known as 'Railway Eshwar'.

People believed that if one prayed to him offering the *bilwapathra* with all devotion, their wishes would certainly be granted. However, Eshwar, that is Shiva, expected nothing in return because he is one god who loves his devotees unconditionally.

Vandana, not to be left behind, told Shrimati enthusiastically, 'Hey Shrimati, I will also pray to Railway Eshwar. If you come first, I shall perform a special puja for him. He will listen, he is a very powerful god.'

Shrimati smiled at her friends' affectionate expressions and said, 'Shari, Vandana, why are you praying to different gods? Should I get the first rank only to beat Shrikant? One should study well to acquire more knowledge. An examination is not the ultimate measure of one's intelligence . . . Have any of you ever asked me how I wrote this essay that has more information than the textbook? I had actually referred to different books on Ashoka, Buddhism, etc. For me, Ashoka is really a great person and I respect and admire him. I would rather spend more time learning about him than studying just to get more marks than Shrikant!'

Her words upset both her friends. They had been praying so hard, and it seemed all a waste! 'Forget it, Shari, let us not pray for Shrimati. We thought that she is on our side. But it looks like she is on Shrikant's side. She is Shrimati Shrikant Deshpande after all. Ultimately they are two sides of the same coin. We are the outsiders,' Vandana muttered, peeved.

Shrimati was about to say something but she didn't. Her name *was* Shrimati Shrikant Deshpande, and that's what caused her all the problems. *Mrs Shrikant Deshpande.*

Who says 'What's in a name?' Here, everything was in the name!

Before the reorganization of the states in 1956, the districts of Dharwad, Karwar, Belgaum and Bijapur were part of the Bombay Presidency. As a result, these districts bear a greater similarity to the culture of Maharashtra than to the traditions of the erstwhile Mysore State in the south. When they were all unified to form the state of Karnataka, these four districts were referred to as North Karnataka. Even though Kannada is the common language of the state, the language of Dharwad and the other three districts has its own accent, intonation and even vocabulary.

Bijapur, home of the famous Gol Gumbaz, one of the largest domes in the world, is known for its salubrious climate, fertile land and tasty produce. There is a Kannada proverb that says, 'Once the Doni halla is full of water, the streets of Bijapur are full of jowar.' Then for the next four to five years, people didn't have to worry about the crops.

Karwar is on the west coast and rich in natural resources. The Sahyadri mountains tower over the region.

Belgaum, situated on the border of Maharashtra and Karnataka, has a lot of Maharashtrian influence and is extremely cultured.

But Dharwad stands apart. It is a city of hills, education and music. Great exponents of the Kirana gharana belong to this town, it is home to some of the oldest educational institutions, and is known for its peace-loving, literate people. There was a time when people in Karnataka said,

'If you throw a stone in Dharwad, it will hit either a musician or a writer.'

Though Hubli is only twenty-two kilometres away, it does not possess the serenity of Dharwad. It is more of a bustling commercial centre for cotton and red chilli trade, among other things.

In the olden days, some families from this region had helped the Peshwas of Maharashtra. As a token of appreciation they were given some lands in the area. Having hereditary ownership, these lands were passed from one generation to the next. As a result, the landlords had different titles and over a period of time, the titles became the surnames of those families, like, Deshpande, Jahagirdar, Inamdar, Desai.

Until a few decades back, these landlords, including the Deshpandes, used to own vast lands which were tilled by the landless labour they employed. Most of the time the landlords did not even visit their fields. And yet, the people who had worked for them for years could never hope to own even a tiny piece of the land. Since they considered themselves aristocrats, the landowners did not believe in working. They spent their time indulging themselves in all sorts of bad habits. It was a purely patriarchal society where the head of the family decided everything—be it arranging a marriage, making a donation to a temple or an ordinary household matter. The women were always in the background, suppressed, and subservient, irrespective of their age.

After India got independence and land reforms were introduced, most of these landowners lost much of their property. Suddenly they found their incomes drastically reduced, and their existence, that of the lower middle class. They had not cultivated; neither did they know any skills

Sudha Murty

nor were they used to hard work. But their family pride, arrogance and ego remained as before. They were like a torn Banaras saree.

Though Shrimati and Shrikant had such a common cultural background, their temperaments were very different. Once upon a time their families had everything, but today they had nothing more than a huge ancestral house and a few pieces of land. They found it hard to maintain the old house, but they couldn't abandon it and live elsewhere. It was an issue of family prestige.

Though they were neighbours, their forefathers always fought like cats and dogs, at the slightest provocation. Actually it was their mountain-like egos that was responsible for the continued enmity.

Another bone of contention was that the two families belonged to different sects—one family worshipped Shiva and was called Smartha, the other was a Vishnu devotee and hence, Vaishnava. While this was not an issue for the men, it was a major factor for the women to fight. The end result was that there was no communication at all between the two families.

Shrimati's grandmother Rindakka should have been born in a kshatriya, or warrior family, for she was extremely aggressive. She was ready to fight with anybody, anytime, anywhere! She did not even require a reason, because she disagreed with everything. People used to say that her poor husband Bindappa could not put up with his wife and so had died at an early age.

But the truth was that Bindappa had died because he was old and had been a slave of many vices. Although he was rich, he was arrogant, uneducated and chauvinistic. Rindakka was his third wife. They had only one son,

Shrikant. Rindakka had become a widow at a very young age and probably that had made her frustrated and irritable. Though she was uneducated, she was an intelligent lady.

Shrikant grew up like his father but with an education. He was not very bright, and extremely lazy. It took him several years to complete his degree course, and when he did, no one would give him a job. He was not too keen to find one either. So, he stayed in Hubli though he was jobless! His daily routine was to wake up anytime after 10 a.m., play cards, get home and relax. Never in his life had he earned a single paisa. Rindakka had hoped that marriage would make him responsible.

As is customary in North Karnataka, a marriage alliance would not go beyond the four districts. It is very unlikely that one marries across the Tungabhadra. Hence, from the neighbouring city of Dharwad the educated Kamala was chosen.

By the time Kamala came to her husband's house, all the lands had disappeared due to the Tenancy Act. Though the economic situation became very delicate the pride and arrogance of the family remained intact. Sensitive Kamala gauged the situation quickly and took up a teaching job at a local school. She was the sole breadwinner for the family now. But still, Rindakka would show her authority as a mother-in-law and utter pungent words that would hurt her. Kamala, an introvert, never said anything. She neither looked down upon her husband nor defied her mother-in-law.

After many years of Shrikant and Kamala's marriage, Shrimati was born and indeed, she brought a change in their lives. Though Shrikantrao Deshpande paid no attention to his wife, he would always be concerned about his daughter.

Shrimati grew up with a jobless father, a domineering grandmother and a timid, loving mother. Kamala took

Sudha Murty

utmost care to bring Shrimati up with strong values and a good education. Shrimati inherited her love for literature from her mother and even as a child spoke pure Kannada. But she would argue with her grandmother and also question her father. She grew up a bright, extremely accommodating but introverted young girl.

Her neighbour Shrikant Deshpande had a different story.

Shrikant's family were Smarthas. His father Raghanna Deshpande was a shade better than his neighbour Shrikant Deshpande. But he died when his son was still in middle school. He had been a clerk at the post office. Gangakka, his wife, was a cunning, manipulative, fierce and an extremely practical lady. Raghanna had left behind two children. The elder child, Rama, was an average-looking girl and not at all a good student, whereas the younger one, Shrikant, was good-looking and very intelligent. He was the apple of his mother's eye! She had pinned all her dreams on him.

Normally, quarrels would arise between Rindakka and Gangakka, the difference in age being no barrier. Gangakka was actually Kamala's age but because of her reticent nature, Kamala didn't fight with anybody.

Gangakka had an older brother, Sheenappa. He was a sweet-talker but a very shrewd man. He was the only one who had stood by Gangakka when her husband passed away. No one but himself had known the reason then. He had four ugly daughters and he had an eye on Shrikant, hoping that at some point in time, he would be able to get Shrikant to marry one of his daughters. Otherwise, he was not a man to help a single person without a vested interest.

Rama took longer than usual to complete her degree. As she was not good-looking, it was a little difficult to find a groom for her. With great difficulty, Sheenappa finally found one and soon, Rama was happily married. When she gave birth to a son, it was treated like quite an achievement. Gangakka felt that her daughter was very fortunate.

Shrikant was unlike his sister Rama who had inherited all the bad qualities of their mother. But Shrikant was focused on his studies and didn't care about the rivalry between the two families, or Sheenappa's role in their lives.

In the space between the two houses, there was a bakula tree. The bakula is about the size of a neem tree and has a lovely canopy of dark green leaves. The tree lives for at least a hundred years, and the more it rains, the more flowers it bears. The bakula flower is very unusual—it is tiny, pale greenish-brown in colour, and is shaped like a crown. As flowers go, it is unattractive, but it has a divine fragrance. Even when the flowers dry and become brown the mild fragrance remains. When the tree is in bloom, the flowers form a carpet on the ground beneath it. The bakula flower is a favourite of the gods too!

It was May end and the hot summer of Hubli was coming to an end. The ripe fruits on the mango tree hinted the end of the mango season. Farmers eagerly awaited Shravan, the rainy season—a season that brings happiness to nature as well as human beings. There are so many poems written and sung about Shravan in Dharwad. It is indeed an inspiration for poets, but a hurdle for young mothers and the aged!

The bakula tree stood gracefully, as usual, spreading its fragrance. It was evening, and the flowers lay on the ground, forming a carpet of blossoms.

Gangakka Deshpande had a small house in a big compound. She and her husband had wanted to extend it once they became prosperous, but unfortunately that never happened. Though Gangakka had a bitter tongue, she was hardworking. She did not waste her time after she finished her cooking. She had made a beautiful garden, with many flowering bushes and vegetable plants. It was a part of her ritual to wake up early in the morning, pick flowers and make a garland, to offer at the temple of Railway Eshwar. This was irrespective of the season. She believed that this kind of deed would bring prosperity and happiness to her children.

But Gangakka was very unhappy about one thing, and that was the bakula tree. It stood exactly in the middle of the common compound of the two houses, indicating that it belonged to both of them. Not only did it give flowers, it also gave the best shade. And that's what made Gangakka angry. Nothing would grow in that shade. She thought the tree was a nuisance, that it took up a lot of space. In Gangakka's dictionary, everything was measured in terms of usefulness. Be it a human being or some material. So, the tree became a bone of contention between the two families. She would keep telling her neighbour to cut off the tree so that she could grow more plants and get some sunshine too.

Shrikant's room faced the bakula tree. Throughout the year, the mild scent of the bakula wafted in through his window. He had developed a special attachment to these flowers and so he opposed his mother's idea of cutting the tree.

On the other side, nobody except Shrimati had the time to tend the garden. Her father, Shrikantrao Deshpande, had no time for any work, let alone looking after the bakula tree. Kamala would always be busy with her school work and Rindakka was an old woman.

Rindakka did not want to cut the tree, not because she loved bakulas, but because Gangakka wanted to. In spite of the battle between these two fierce women, the bakula continued to bloom every day.

It was the day the tenth standard board exam results were to be announced. After the last exam Shrimati had told her mother that she had done fairly well. She was not the kind who would exaggerate, be it success or disappointment.

Shrikant had told his mother that he had done extremely well and was also expecting a rank.

More than Shrimati, her friends who had bet on many things, were worried. Even the teachers were wondering what rank Shrimati and Shrikant would get. They were undoubtedly the most talented students in the school. Either way, the school would get the credit for getting a rank. At home, Gangakka and Rindakka were waiting to know the results too.

Shrimati was the only one who was not at all perturbed. She was neither bent upon doing better than Shrikant nor did she look upon her success as a matter of family honour and pride. It was true that she was brighter than Shrikant, but exam results did not always reflect or depend upon intelligence.

Though Shrimati was so young, she had the equanimity of an ascetic. Over the years, she had sometimes scored more marks than Shrikant, at others he had beaten her scores. She had taken it in her stride. So, that day's outcome did not hold any anxiety for her. But Shrikant was restless and impatient for the results. Holding a bakula in his palm, he was wondering why he was fascinated by this tiny flower. The flower was neither as beautiful as a rose nor had the fragrance of a jasmine or champaka. And yet, it was always very special to him. It held an inexplicable attraction for him.

Shrikant remembered many ancient stories that connected the bakula with romance. It seems in the olden days, when young men travelled far distances for many days, they would carry small objects in memory of their loved ones. The bakula flower was one such memento that these young men carried, because, even though it would dry up, it would still give out the same fragrance, like the beloved's love.

Without realizing it, Shrikant had come to associate the bakula flower with Shrimati. It is true that they hardly ever spoke to each other, but it was equally true that there was a strange attraction between them. Perhaps it was their age—adolescence—or the teasing of their friends or just the way their names conjugated! Of course, it was Shrikant who was more attracted towards Shrimati than she was to him. Though Shrikant was the more extroverted of the two, and he often wondered what was in Shrimati's mind, he wasn't outspoken enough to ask her.

Only Shrikant and Gangakka were at home. Gangakka was aware that the results were due to come and so she thought she would light ghee lamps to please the gods. There was a lot of ghee at home and since Shrikant would not eat it, Gangakka used it for the lamps.

There was a knock on the door and when Gangakka saw it was the postman bearing a telegram, she became very nervous. It reminded her of her husband's death. For her, a telegram would always bring bad news. Holding the telegram in her hand, she prayed to god to forgive her for using the rancid ghee and promised that she would use the fresh one, if this telegram did not turn out to bear bad news!

In a trembling voice, she called Shrikant and handed the telegram to him. 'Shrikant, here is a telegram. See whether it is from Byadagi?'

Byadagi was the small village where her daughter Rama stayed with her husband, Krishna. Gangakka could think only of her daughter. Her horizon was extremely limited.

Shrikant was equally curious to know what it was. He opened it quickly, glanced through it and said to his mother in a delighted voice, 'Avva, this telegram is from the Bangalore SSLC Board. I have stood second in the entire Board.'

Gangakka did not understand what that meant. All she was interested in was whether he was first in the school.

'Shrikant, are you first in the school or not? Have you scored more than Shrimati? Who has taken the first place?'

Shrikant smiled at his mother's ignorance.

'Avva, I have stood second in the entire state and ought to be first in the Hubli Centre and of course our school. I don't know about Shrimati, but she wouldn't have scored more than me! You know, now I can get a full scholarship and you need not struggle for my education.'

Shrikant was very happy indeed.

Gangakka remembered her late husband and her eyes became moist.

'Shrikant, Lord Mylaralinga has blessed us. He has always been kind to you . . .'

But Shrikant was still getting used to the idea of having done so well. He had never expected to get the second rank. At the most, he was expecting to be one among the first twenty. Now he was most curious as to who had got the first rank. It must be someone from Mysore or Bangalore, he thought.

Then his thoughts turned to Shrimati. What rank had she got? A tap on his shoulder shook him out of his reverie.

Sudha Murty

He turned around to see his teacher Mr Kulkarni. He was beaming with pride. His usual paan-stained mouth was unusually clean that day. In his happiness he seemed to have forgotten to eat his paan.

Thumping Shrikant on his back, he said, 'Shrikant, you both have made a record! In the entire history of the school, such a thing has not happened. The Board has informed us that Shrimati has stood first, and you second! You have given us a wonderful reward for having taught you! Generally, the first and second ranks do not go to the same school. But we have been fortunate to be the first school to get the top two places in the same year . . .'

Shrikant's mind went numb. Mr Kulkarni's chatter continued, but Shrikant did not hear a word. Had a thunderbolt struck him or had he touched a live wire?

He couldn't believe what Mr Kulkarni had told him. His bubble of happiness vanished and he was close to tears. But he controlled himself. Men were not supposed to shed tears in front of others!

He felt like Arjuna in the Mahabharata who was so focused on his archery skills that if he ever missed his aim, he suffered unbearable agony.

Just then Gangakka came in and told Kulkarni Sir that he must at least have some sweets since he had brought the good news. But he said that he wanted to go and see Shrimati and that he would come back later.

Absent-mindedly Shrikant said namaskar to his teacher and went back to his own thoughts. His mind was pricking him: Shrikant Deshpande, you have missed your target. You had dismissed Shrimati as a mere girl, but silently and soberly that girl has given you a powerful answer! She has shown you what she is capable of. Shrikant tried to analyse the reason for his unhappiness and disappointment. What had gone wrong?

Actually, nothing had gone wrong. The cause for his disappointment was her success. Though he had scored more marks than he had expected or hoped for, Shrimati had scored more than him. Was he ever going to be free of this Shrimati? Would she always be a challenge to him, and in her calm, smiling way, defeat him? What would he say to Ravi and Mallesh now, after boasting to them that he was smarter than her?

Shrikant's gaze turned involuntarily to Shrimati's house. He could see Shrimati, dressed as usual in a cotton saree, a string of bakula flowers tucked in her long plait her only adornment. She was engrossed in a conversation with her friends Sharada and Vandana.

What were they talking about? Were they laughing at his defeat? Was she gloating over her success? Shrikant was getting more and more agitated.

Just then he saw his group of friends led by Mallesh and Ravi approaching his house. Mallesh had a garland in his hand. Shrikant went out to meet them and Mallesh garlanded him. Then in a low tone he said, 'Congratulations, Shrikant! She may be first but you are first among the boys.'

Shaking hands with Shrikant, Ravi said, 'Come on, Mallya, did we know that Shrikant would get the second rank? This is indeed a bonus for us. So what if Shrikant has not got the first rank this time? He will definitely get it next time. Haven't you heard the famous poem, "*Try and try again boys, you will succeed at last.*"'

Mallya laughed, 'Yes, yes, that poem is especially written for boys.'

Patting Ravi on the back, he said, 'Now, let's not be jealous. Isn't she our classmate too? Has she not brought glory to our school? As far as I can see, we have made a lot of fun of her but she hasn't retaliated even once. We should go and congratulate her. Shrikant you must also come. I am sure there will not be any problem.'

Shrimati had been surprised to see the telegram informing her about her first rank. She had never ever expected that! When her mother had asked her about her performance in the exam, she had casually said that she had done fairly well. This first rank made her really happy, but she kept her cool.

Actually, it was her friends who were absolutely thrilled, particularly Sharada, because Shrimati's success was a one-up in the girls' camp and one-down in the boys' camp.

Rindakka, who had looked down upon Shrimati all these years beause she was not as fair and good-looking as herself, was very pleased that her granddaughter had done better than her neighbour's son! Suddenly her tone changed. 'After all she is my granddaughter,' she said with pride in her voice, 'she has inherited my intelligence.'

Shrimati's father Shrikant Deshpande, too, was beaming with happiness and was very proud of his daughter's performance. He behaved as though he was responsible for it. Kamala had a look of peace and satisfaction on her face. But in Shrimati, there was absolutely no change.

When Shrimati saw the group of her classmates coming towards her house, she wondered what they wanted, what would happen. She wasn't curious to know Shrikant's marks. Though not first rank, she was sure he would have also got very good marks.

She quickly warned her friends and the people at home not to say anything to Shrikant. 'After all, an examination is not the index in life. It is just a matter of luck at that moment. I do not want to hurt anybody when they come to our house,' she said.

Sharada was most displeased with this remark.

The rainy season had set in. There was a continuous drizzle. Mother earth was so thirsty that she had been longing for the showers. The dried yellow grass was turning green. Flowers bloomed and were looking fresh as if after a bath. The beautiful champaka flowers shivered in the cold breeze. The bakula tree was so happy that it was laden with blossoms. Though it was not pouring, the continuous drizzle was making life difficult for everyone. Even Gangakka was tired of picking up the bakula flowers and making innumerable garlands for all the gods.

Almost a week passed by in celebrations and felicitations after the announcement of the results. There was great jubilation in Shrimati's school because of the two ranks that the school had bagged. With this result, the school's reputation got a huge boost and there was a long queue of parents when new admissions were announced.

Shrimati and Shrikant were the focus of all the attention. They were given numerous prizes, much praise was heaped upon them by their teachers and students looked upon them as role models.

In all these felicitations, neither Shrimati nor Shrikant congratulated or even spoke to each other. Though Shrimati tried once or twice, Shrikant did not respond. He was still too hurt. So Shrimati withdrew. It was not proper for a girl to push too much. In a place like Hubli, such things mattered a lot. Girls were not supposed to even talk to boys in public.

After the excitement had died down, Shrimati decided to go and visit her maternal grandmother who lived in Dharwad. She was too old to travel, so the granddaughter thought she would go and get her blessings.

Shrimati took the Hubli–Dharwad local train. After the office rush hour, the train was usually empty. Shrimati got into a deserted compartment and sat by a window. Since it was quite a boring journey, she had brought a book along and as soon as she settled down, opened it and started reading. Just as the train was about to start, Shrimati realized that one more person had entered the compartment and occupied the seat opposite hers. She looked up and to her surprise, found it was her classmate Shrikant Deshpande.

For a minute, she was taken aback, but she said nothing.

Shrikant was equally surprised to see Shrimati. He was travelling to Dharwad to meet his sister's in-laws. When he looked at Shrimati, he did not know what to do. This was the first time both of them were facing each other without their respective friends. Shrikant was quick to observe that she was simply dressed as usual, with no jewellery except the glass bangles on her hands and the string of his favourite bakula flowers tucked in her hair.

The mild fragrance of bakula pervaded the compartment. He looked at her face and saw she had a natural smile, which was neither ingratiating nor condescending. Shrikant mustered up enough courage to talk to her.

'Are you going to Dharwad?' he asked, knowing very well that the train's destination was only Dharwad!

'Yes, to meet my grandmother. She lives in Malmaddi. What about you?'

'I am going to meet some relatives in Saptapur.' The conversation stopped there.

Although Shrikant was gregarious by nature, that day he did not know what to say, even though he really wanted to talk to her. He felt drawn to Shrimati, but could not say why. Perhaps because they were opposites in nature, or because she was his rival or because forbidden fruit is always more desirable!

Suddenly he remembered he had not congratulated her, so he extended his hand and said, 'Congratulations.'

Shrimati was confused for a moment. A gesture, like shaking hands with a man, was not common in the society of that time.

However, she reluctantly took his hand and shyly said, 'Thanks and congratulations to you also.'

'Why are you congratulating me? For having stood second, is it?'

'No, Shrikant. Believe me, I think your success is more deserved than mine. There is no great difference between the first and second rank. It is only a matter of the examiner's mood and a few better answers. Many a time I wanted to talk to you, and tell you how much I appreciate the qualities you have which I don't. You are so focused and hardworking. Over a period of time, these qualities will fetch you whatever your want. Unlike you, I am happy with small things . . .'

Shrikant was surprised by her words and happy too. A girl who was brighter than him had appreciated his qualities. He felt elated! Suddenly he knew how the conversation could continue.

'Shrimati, which college are you going to join?'

'I have decided to take up arts.'

That meant Shrimati would not be a classmate any more. More than that she would no longer be his rival! The thought cheered him up. 'Why do you want to take up arts when you are so good at science?'

'I am more inclined towards history and literature. Moreover, I have a principle of my own. We should do what we really like. For two things in life it is very important for us to make our own decisions. One is education. I believe we must study only that subject which we like.'

'What about the other one?'

'The other one is marriage, because partners remain with each other forever in life. Other things like choosing a saree or buying a house can be reversed. But not these two things.'

Shrikant agreed immediately, as long as she was taking a different stream!

But he was really puzzled. It was very unusual of shy Shrimati to talk so frankly. Shrimati too began to feel uncomfortable because her hand was still in Shrikant's hand! He had not left it. Gathering up her courage she said softly, 'Will you let go of my hand, please?'

Shrikant quickly dropped it and looked very embarrassed. He hadn't realized how long he had been holding on to her hand.

The train had now reached Amargol station and there was no signal to go ahead. So the train had to halt there. It was going to be late reaching Dharwad.

Shrikant felt that this was a good opportunity to get to know Shrimati. Already he had realized that she was so different from what he had imagined. Whatever she said, it was simple, straight, clear and directly from the heart. There was no artifice, no attempt to show off, nothing put on. Much as he didn't like to admit it, he knew that she was definitely more intelligent than him.

And all this while, he had been hearing only negative remarks about her from his sister and mother. Perhaps, they were not even aware of her true nature.

How would anyone know her without becoming friends with her?

'Shrimati, now our paths will be different and our friends will be different too. In our school we could hardly speak because of our names. Now onwards, let us be good friends and talk to each other.'

Shrimati looked into Shrikant's eyes. She liked this straightforward, good-natured boy, she decided. What was the harm in being friends?

'Where can we meet and talk? You know the background of our families. My grandmother and your mother are always around. I cannot meet you outside,' Shrimati's face was troubled.

'Don't worry, Shrimati. Every problem has a solution. And this is not a great problem at all. You know that every morning my mother goes to the Railway Eshwar temple and it takes her at least an hour to go there and come back. Your grandmother also goes to the Rayara Mattha at the same time. That is the best time for us to meet and talk.'

Shrimati was surprised at Shrikant's observation. Even she was not aware of such details.

'But where can we meet?'

'God is kind to us. We have a bakula tree in common. Early in the morning, the flowers are freshly fallen. You can come to collect them and so will I. Is it not a right place?'

Shrimati liked Shrikant's strategy and nodded her head with a smile.

Shrimati, Vandana and Sharada joined the arts college while Shrikant, Ravi and Mallesh joined the science college.

Two months later, Mallesh, finding the science course tough, joined the commerce college. Since the classmates had all gone different ways, no one teased Shrikant or Shrimati any more.

Shrimati loved the college more than her school. It had an excellent library and she could borrow the best books from there. As her classes were in the morning, she was free during the afternoons. So she was able to help her mother at home and have enough time to study and read. Kamala would have liked her daughter to study medicine, but she did not say anything knowing her daughter's inclination towards history. Shrikantrao wanted his daughter to become a lawyer but he dared not say anything to her, knowing her scant respect for him.

Shrikant and Shrimati would meet every day near the bakula tree, and talk about various things. Shrimati would diligently gather the bakula flowers, while Shrikant would talk about his college and his dreams.

During one such conversation, Shrikant told her, 'Shrimati, I don't like you calling me Shrikant like everybody else. I want you to call me *Shri*.'

For a moment Shrimati did not understand what he meant. But when she realized it, she blushed and nodded her head.

No one in either house was aware of their 'flower-gathering meetings'.

The two years of Pre University passed without any difficulties. And so did their friendship.

Shrikant had grown more confident and mature. He did very well in the exams and got a good rank. With his marks, he could get admission in any of the engineering colleges in Karnataka. But he had decided to sit for the entrance test for IIT. Of the five premier technology institutes in India, the Indian Institute of Technology, Bombay was his first choice since it was closest to home. But he was taking a big chance. The entrance test was tough and the competition was stiff.

Ravi Patil also decided to join Shrikant in preparing for the entrance test.

Shrikant met one of their seniors, Vasudev Shenoy, who had gone to IIT three years ago, and got all the information and tips on how to prepare. He was determined to get into IIT. Both Ravi and Shrikant had financial problems but that did not deter Shrikant from his ambition. He told his mother to sell a part of the land if needed. Their friend Mallesh also did fairly well in his commerce college.

Shrimati, whose favourite subjects were history, sanskrit and english, had joined the arts college for a BA degree, much to everyone's surprise. She was known as an extremely bright student, so other students pointed to her saying, 'See, that's Shrimati Deshpande. Though she stood first in the Board she has joined the arts college!' Shrimati would smile to herself.

Her friend Sharada's family wanted her to get a BA degree. The subject did not matter. A degree was a rare thing in their family. Vandana's father wanted her to do an MA, like he had done.

Sudha Murty

Even after they joined college, there was no change in Shrimati's daily routine. She, Vandana and Sharada went to college together as they had gone to school.

Though she was very frank and friendly with these two girls, she had not told them of her daily meetings with Shrikant. In fact, she had not wanted to share it with anybody. She could not explain why.

Soon the IIT results were announced. Shrikant and Ravi both got through, and secured admission to IIT, Bombay. Shrikant even got the subject of his choice, computer science, unlike Ravi who had wanted mechanical but got metallurgy.

Shrikant was going to stay away from Hubli for the first time in his life, and he was feeling a little uneasy. He would have to stay in Bombay for the next five years. He was sure that he would miss the early morning meetings under the bakula tree. In the last two years he had developed a strong attachment for 'his Shrimati'. It was more than an adolescent crush, he knew. She was very special to him.

Shrimati was sad too. Like Shrikant, she had also got used to meeting him in the mornings. Now, for the next five years, that would not be possible. Though he would come home twice every year, the long absence could change his mind, she thought. What if he met some smart bright girls in Bombay? Would his affection for her remain the same? When ravishing gladioli and fragrant rajanigandhas were around, would he remember the tiny, self-effacing bakula?

The day of their last meeting dawned. Shrimati did not say anything, but she was pale. Shrikant knew she was upset—he could read her mind.

'Shrimati,' he said to her in an assuring voice, 'you know that I am highly focused. I am going there only for studies. I will look neither to the left nor to the right. Nothing matters to me. I am and will always be your Shri.'

'Will you write to me, Shri?'

'Of course I will write. In the second and fourth week of every month. And you must write to me every first and third week.'

Shrimati could say nothing more. She lowered her head and bent down to pick up the delicate bakula flowers. Shrikant said to her, 'Shrimati, I'll miss your company and our flower.'

'Then I will enclose a flower in every letter,' Shrimati promised.

Both of them were so engrossed in their conversation, they had forgotten that they had crossed the time limit. Rindakka was back from the temple. Not seeing Shrimati in the kitchen, she had started yelling.

'Shrimati, where are you? The milk is boiling.'

Shrimati was startled.

'Shri, I have to run now. When will we meet again?'

Smilingly Shrikant said, 'In December. But tell me, Shrimati, to which address can I send the letters?'

'There is always a solution to every problem, haven't you told me? Write to my address but don't write your address at the back. Nobody will come to know.'

Shrimati disliked such deceitful methods but in her circumstances, she had no choice.

Neither had Shrikant travelled much nor had he had much exposure to the outside world. Since all his relatives lived in and around Dharwad, he had not got the opportunity to go anywhere else. Only after joining IIT did Shrikant get to meet and know about people from different parts of the country.

IIT, Bombay had a sprawling campus. It was located in Powai, a suburb of Bombay. The atmosphere inside the institute was a stark contrast to the crowded, bustling city outside. The campus had a lot of greenery, and the many buildings—offices, classrooms, labs, auditorium, canteen, hostels—were spread out over a large area. There was no distraction; it was an ideal place for studies. There were very few girls in the engineering course. Whenever Shrikant came across a girl in the campus, he would think of Shrimati. With her intelligence and capacity for hard work, she would have definitely got a place in IIT. He often imagined what life would have been like if Shrimati was also there.

At first Shrikant was very homesick. He missed his family. He felt a misfit in the cosmopolitan crowd. But as the days passed he began to enjoy the course, he made friends and got used to the food. All his classmates, no matter where they came from, what language they spoke, were there because they were really bright, and very focused. Before long, he found he was happy in IIT.

As he had promised, he wrote to Shrimati every second and fourth week of the month, and shared all his feelings with her. He described in his letters the course he was doing, the food in the hostel mess, the new friends he had made. Through his words, he introduced her to their world, and to the charms of Bombay. Shrimati, on the other hand, did not have much to say. There was no great change in her life. Yet she replied regularly to his letters every first and third week of the month. She never forgot to enclose a bakula flower. Whenever Shrikant received her letters, he felt as if Shrimati was standing next to him, the gentle, mildly fragrant, homely but extremely affectionate Shrimati!

One day, as he was holding the bakula in his hand, he suddenly realized why the flower meant so much to him. The bakula was now, for him, a symbol of Shrimati, a personification of her!

Shrikant collected all the bakula flowers in a small bag and placed it beneath his pillow. He knew that the scent from the flowers would not fade with time.

Time marched on. Shrimati completed her BA degree successfully, getting two gold medals in her subject. Sharada Emmikeri managed to get through, while Vandana passed with a second class. The next step was to apply for an MA course at Karnataka University, Dharwad. Vandana opted for political science and Shrimati for history.

The two friends commuted to the university every day, covering the twenty-five kilometre distance by the university bus rather than by the local train. Both of them enjoyed the ride and used the time to compare notes on their respective courses and classmates. Shrimati was eagerly looking forward to Dr Rao, the present Vice-Chancellor, returning to his parent history department the following year. She had heard so much about his brilliance as a scholar and his wonderful teaching skills that she was confident he would inspire her to give her best to the subject.

However, they did miss their friend Sharada.

As promised, Shrikant visited Hubli every December but in the summer holidays he would take up training with different companies to get practical experience and greater exposure. Only the last ten days of his vacation, which invariably coincided with the beginning of the month of Shravan, would he spend in Hubli. Those days were for Shrimati.

Gangakka looked forward to Shrikant's visits too. She would cook a variety of dishes to make up for the time her son missed home food. She believed that he came home to be with her. Gangakka never dreamt that it was Shrimati who drew him to Hubli and that it was her he yearned to see.

Now, although they could meet at the University campus, they continued the ritual of their early morning chat under the bakula tree. The tree, sole witness to their conversations, smiled indulgently on them.

Vandana soon came to know about Shrikant and Shrimati's friendship. But she did not mention it to anybody. She knew that if Gangakka found out, the consequences would be serious.

Whenever Shrikant came to the University to meet Shrimati, Vandana would return to Hubli alone. If Rindakka asked why Shrimati hadn't returned, Vandana would cover up for her friend and say, 'She is studying in the library.'

Shrimati found University much more exciting than college. She learned that history is not merely concerned with men or a nation. Everything had a history. Music, dance, art and even history had a history. Gradually she developed a fine critical sensibility and trained herself to think logically and reduce emotional idealism. By the end of the first term itself she understood the importance of field visits. They made everything she read in textbooks come alive. The department organized many such trips as a result of which Shrimati saw a number of historic places. She was amazed to find how a country's present culture depended on its past history.

The well-mannered Shrimati endeared herself to her teachers and classmates alike. The professors were delighted to have an intelligent student like her in the history department.

In the meantime, Vandana's life was taking a new turn. As she was neither a very bright student, nor keen on a career, her parents were planning to get her married. They found an eligible young man, Pramod, an engineer working with Larsen & Toubro, a well-known company, in Bombay. Pramod was originally from Belgaum. He was the only son of his parents and they owned a small house in Bombay. Since he did not have any family commitments, was well qualified and held a good job, he was most eligible in the marriage market.

As per tradition, the two horoscopes were matched and Pramod came to see Vandana with his family. He liked her and the marriage was finalized.

By then Vandana was in the final year of her MA, so both sets of parents decided that the marriage would take place after her exams. But after Pramod came to Hubli a few times to meet her, Vandana lost interest in her studies!

Shrimati was curious to know what Vandana and Pramod talked about. Theirs was an arranged marriage, they did not know each other, so what did they say to each other?

'Vandana, what do you talk about with Pramod? You don't even know him.'

'What do you speak with Shrikant for hours together?' Vandana countered.

'Well, he was our classmate. Moreover, we have been good friends for a long time.'

'Oh, don't give me that explanation! It is not mere friendship. Ask yourself. Nobody spends such long hours, without telling people at home, with just a friend!'

Shrimati fell silent. Suddenly she began to feel a strange loneliness. It was not that she had not thought of marriage. But now she could not think of anyone other than Shrikant for a husband.

Having seen her incompatible parents and the kind of family life they led she was sure she would only marry a person who would understand her feelings and have consideration for her, unlike her father who only thought of himself all the time.

Although Shrikant and she were close friends, the issue of marriage had not yet come up. She felt there was something between them that went beyond friendship. Even if she had not shown any emotion outwardly, in her heart she was quite attached to Shrikant. What was on his mind, she wondered.

While it was natural for her to think of marriage—she was of marriageable age after all—Shrikant could not think of anything other than completing his B.Tech. and getting a good job. Marriage was far, far away.

In one of her usual letters she casually mentioned Vandana's engagement.

One day after the December vacations, when exams were round the corner and Shrimati was busy with her seminars, Shrikant surprised Shrimati with an untimely visit to Hubli. Shrimati was overjoyed.

They decided Shrikant would wait for Shrimati near the town clock tower till she finished her seminar. 'Shri,' she said to him, 'I do not have class today. Shall we go to Atthikolla? It is not hot outside.'

Atthikolla was a picnic spot in Dharwad, known for its mango groves. At this time of the year, early February, all the trees were covered with tender, new leaves, reddish green in colour. It was a very pleasant season—winter was over and the heat of summer was yet to begin.

Usually Shrikant would never disagree with Shrimati in such matters. But that day he said, 'No, let's go to Thackeray Park.'

'Call it Chennamma Park,' exclaimed Shrimati, her sense of history prompting her outburst.

Centuries ago, the British collector of Dharwad, a man called Thackeray, had fought a battle with Chennamma, the queen of Kittur. The officer had lost his life. The British erected a memorial in his name and built a park. Before independence, it was known as Thackeray Park. But after independence, the patriotic people of Dharwad called it Chennamma Park because it was Queen Chennamma who had killed Thackeray in the battlefield.

'It's all the same. Will the place change with the name? Let's go.' Shrikant was not bothered about such things.

Vandana, having seen them from a distance, went back to Hubli alone. Shrikant and Shrimati went to Thackeray or Kittur Chennamma Park. It was opposite the Mental Hospital on the Hubli–Belgaum Road. There were very few people in the garden and most of them were sleeping, using their hand as a pillow.

They chose a big banyan tree and sat beneath its sprawling branches.

Shrimati was in great spirits. Not only had her seminar gone off very well, she'd also had this surprise visit from Shrikant. She was chattering continuously, while the normally talkative Shrikant was in deep thought. Shrimati did not notice anything amiss.

Sudha Murty

'Shri, today I had a seminar and everyone appreciated my work. I spoke on Ashoka. Do you remember? I had written an essay when we were in tenth standard. Today, I can write better. That time, I had less access to books and I was more emotional about Ashoka. Even now, whenever I read about Ashoka, my respect for him grows and he fascinates me. Shri, is the name Ashoka not beautiful? Historians call him Dharmashoka—the virtuous one . . .'

Shrikant interrupted Shrimati and with a mischievous smile asked, 'It seems you like that name a lot. So, if you have a son, will you name him Ashoka?'

Shrimati looked at him with surprise, wondering why the subject of naming an unborn son had come up!

Smilingly she replied, 'Yes! What's wrong with that? I would not think twice before doing it. But since you asked about names, Shri, let me tell you that I also like the name Adityavikrama. Vikramaditya was a title in the old days. Whenever a king achieved something extraordinary through bravery and adventure, he was given the title Vikramaditya. During the Gupta dynasty, Chandragupta II was called Vikramaditya. If I have another son, I will name him Adityavikrama . . .'

Shrimati spoke in all innocence, like a history teacher to her students.

'Shri, Siddhartha Gautama is another person I really admire. He understood the nature of sorrow and knew the true values of life. He gave up his kingdom and his family for the sake of humanity. His message is full of love and compassion. He neither won any war nor did he establish a great empire. However, he won the empire of hearts. Maybe if I have one more son, I will name him Siddhartha Gautama . . .'

Shrikant moved closer to Shrimati, held her hands, and whispered softly but clearly in her ear, 'Shrimati, when I become an engineer, don't you think that it would be too much to ask for Siddhartha Gautama also, on my meagre salary?'

'What?' Shrimati exclaimed flustered, but in a flurry of joy.

Sudha Murty

It was the beginning of March and the University campus was normally deserted. Students were at home, preparing for their examinations, and professors were busy setting question papers. Only those scholars who were doing their Ph.D or some academic research came to the library in the University during this time. For a person like Shrimati, an examination was a cakewalk. So, even in March, she came to the University to help her professors with some project or the other. She enjoyed it and did not mind coming all the way to the campus for this. Vandana was extremely busy preparing for the examination and day-dreaming about her marriage.

One day Shrimati was in the library making notes for her professor who was going to Japan to attend an international seminar on 'Buddhism in India and Japan'.

Shrimati had read so much about Buddhism, how though it had originated in India, it had spread to many countries in South-east Asia. China, Japan and Sri Lanka were all Buddhist countries. And Indonesia, once a Buddhist centre, boasted of one of the great Buddhist monuments, Borobudur. She would have loved to travel to all these places, but financial constraints had made that impossible. However, now that her professor was going to Japan and after that to Indonesia, he would describe it all to her when he returned. Even that was enough for her! While she was thinking these thoughts, the department peon Siddappa came and stood in front of her. 'Madam, Professor is calling you, wants you to come immediately.'

'Why Siddappa, what is it? He knows I am doing some important work!'

'Some white man whom I have never seen before, must be a friend of the professor, has come and they were talking about you . . . maybe that's why they have called you.'

Shrimati was wondering who it could be when she entered her professor's room. There was another person there, an elderly gentleman with grey hair, well built, around six feet tall. He looked at her and gave her a friendly smile.

'Come in Shrimati. Meet my friend Professor Mike Collins,' Professor Rao introduced his guest.

Shrimati could not believe her ears. Any student of history would know his name. If there were a Nobel Prize for history, it would certainly have gone to Professor Collins a long time back.

Many a times Shrimati and the other students had heard Professor Rao talk about Professor Collins. He was an American and came from a very affluent family. His father was a wealthy businessman. But the son had been passionate about history and had gone to Oxford to study. He got his Ph.D from there. His wife Jane, whom he had met at college and later married, was also a historian. They had done some fascinating research work together.

They had a daughter, Dorothy, and she too, like her parents, had chosen history as her subject and was working towards a doctorate.

Unfortunately, Jane had died of cancer recently and Professor Collins was alone. He had been on a tour of Sri Lanka, and on the way back had come to meet his old friend.

Professor Rao had been his student at Yale University and a special affection had developed between the two of them.

Shrimati could see the happiness on Professor Rao's face on seeing his teacher.

'Mike, Shrimati is an excellent student and one of my favourites. Her interest in history is similar to Dorothy's. She has prepared extensive notes on Buddhism. You can see how she writes.'

Shrimati went red, hearing her teacher praise her in front of such a well-known person.

'Hello, Shrimati! It is nice to meet you. I would love to see your notes sometime. I am not an expert on Buddhism like your teacher,' he spoke to her in American accent, which was a little difficult for Shrimati to understand.

Shrimati was embarrassed giving her notes to such a famous person. However, she placed them on the table next to him.

Professor Rao told her, 'Shrimati, Mike had come to visit the Calcutta museum and he has finished much of his work. It was very nice of him to come to this small town to meet me. Though Karnataka has famous historical monuments, he doesn't have enough time to see all of them. But he cannot go back to the US without seeing at least a couple of them. So I have suggested that he should visit Badami, Aihole and Pattadakal. It can be done in one day.'

'Yes, Sir, they are really wonderful places. Every historian will enjoy them.'

'That is why I sent for you. You must accompany him on this tour.'

Shrimati was surprised, 'Why me, Sir? He would like to spend more time with you, I think.'

'I wish I could go with him but someone is coming tomorrow with a marriage proposal for my daughter. And you know that it wouldn't look good if the girl's father is not there! So I want you to take him around. Besides, you are an excellent guide.'

'Who else will come along, Sir?'

'My son Shashi will accompany you. Mike doesn't stand on formalities. After all, it is a one-day trip. My driver will also be with you people.'

While the conversation was still going on between Shrimati and Professor Rao, Professor Collins was going through Shrimati's notes.

She had described beautifully the differences between Vihara and Chaitya, the origin of the Jataka tales and the decline of Buddhism.

After Shrimati had been given instructions for the trip, she left.

Professor Collins turned to Professor Rao and said, 'Her ideas are very clear and logical. She is probably better than Dorothy. No wonder you said she was an excellent student.'

Professor Rao beamed with pride.

The next day, Shashi, Shrimati and Professor Collins left at the break of dawn. As Professor Collins was scared of drinking water in India and he found it difficult to eat the spicy food at the various eating joints, they carried bottled water, fruit and some bread and jam for him. But regular lunch was packed for Shashi and Shrimati.

The staple food of North Karnataka is jowar roti. Another favourite is avalakki, a dish made with beaten rice. There is a saying that if you go to North Karnataka and don't eat avalakki then you've missed something in life. People there are very fond of sweets too.

It was the beginning of March and the sun was not harsh yet. The road was fairly free of traffic, so the morning journey was pleasant.

'Shrimati, my friend said you are an excellent guide. But you don't seem to speak at all! Why don't you tell me the history of this place?' said Professor Collins, with a smile.

'Sir, how can I guide someone like you?'

'Come on, Shrimati! Don't call me Sir. Call me Mike. In America we address everyone by their first name.'

'But Sir, you are older to me in age and more so in knowledge. In our culture, addressing elderly people by their first name is looked upon as rudeness. I can never do that.'

'All right, then, call me whatever you please. Moreover, what's in a name? Now, tell me about the places we are visiting today.'

'Sir, every person grows up with the history of the place to which he or she belongs. Whenever I used to come here as a little girl, my mother would explain to me its importance. She used to tell me that many wars were fought here and many kings had ruled the place. The stone monuments are silent witnesses to many momentous events. At that time, I used to feel happy that my ancestors were a part of the battles and a part of the kingdom too. I still feel that I belong to this area. The events might have taken place twelve centuries back, but when I closed my eyes, I could visualize many things. It made me very emotional. Later, when I grew up, I became passionate about history and started detaching it from the emotional point of view and became more aware of the facts.'

'That's right, Shrimati. It's truly a historian's view. However unpleasant it may be, one should never give up the critical attitude. Where the heart rules, there the mind grows dull.'

'Sir, sorry. I didn't answer your basic question. This area was ruled by the mighty Chalukya dynasty and the place now called Badami was known as Vatapi. The Chalukyas ruled in the eighth century and at that time, this area was very prosperous. There are many stories regarding the origin of this dynasty. The founder's name was Pulakeshi and they say he was nurtured on tiger's milk on top of the hill. From that I conclude that he was a very brave man. The greatest ruler of the Chalukya dynasty was Pulakeshi II. He defeated Harshavardhana, a powerful king of the north, on the banks of the river Narmada . . .'

Shashi, a science student, had been reluctant to come on this historical tour. He would have preferred to spend the day in Dharwad, watching the latest movie. He was bored and kept looking at his watch.

They reached Badami, a sleepy little hamlet. It was no longer like Vatapi, the capital of the glorious Chalukya empire of the past. They parked the car at the bottom of the hills and went up to see the caves.

There are three huge granite hills in the middle of the town. The cave temples are carved out of these hills. Probably, this is one of the places where the concept of cave temples originated. There are Jain and Hindu cave temples. The steps carved in the hill lead to all the temples.

When seen from top, Badami looks like a village that will never ever wake up, shrivelled in its poverty, having forgotten, forever, its glorious past.

Shrimati explained.

'Sir, when you look at the caves, you can see the pillars and one assumes that the pillars take the weight of the temple. But in reality, that is not true. The pillars are all false pillars. This concept was later copied in many cave temples. You can see Lord Ganapati, the famous deity with a human body and elephant head. He is known as Vatapi Ganapati.'

Professor Collins was observing everything keenly.

Shrimati continued, 'In the olden days, the ceilings of these caves were covered with beautiful paintings. But now they have disappeared due to the lack of protection and ignorance.'

'Shrimati, tell me more about the paintings.'

Shashi realized that if the conversation went on this way, they wouldn't reach Dharwad before midnight. He could not understand why they were talking so much about some invisible paintings. He decided to go sit in a canteen and read a magazine. Saying he would be back in a minute, he slipped away.

Shrimati and Professor Collins did not notice his absence.

'Sir, the technique of this type of painting was unique. It must have been difficult to paint in these caves without proper ventilation and light. The artist really had to struggle to reach the ceiling and paint on it. They used natural vegetable colours, powdered coloured stones, molasses, lime and other material from nature. They would first prepare the surface of the wall using a mixture of earth, powdered stone, some husk like material, molasses and cow dung. They would then apply a coat of lime on it. After it dried they would use the colours and finally polish it smooth. The paintings of the Ajanta caves used the same technique. Among them, the Court of Parameshwara Pulakeshi, the Dark Princess and many other paintings remain as beautiful after all these centuries.'

Shrimati pointed out the sculptures of the eighteen-handed dancing Shiva, the Caves of Mangalesha, and numerous yaksha-yakshinis, the Sleeping Vishnu, and many more artistic depictions.

Before they knew it, lunchtime had long gone by. The sun was a little hotter but the enthusiasm of these two people was not dampened by the temperature or the time.

In spite of his age and the hectic morning Professor Collins's spirits were as high as a teenager's.

They had a late lunch and headed for Aihole and Pattadakal.

Badami, Aihole and Pattadakal are known as the golden triangle of North Karnataka. They are also world heritage sites. The word Pattadakallu means a place where kings were crowned. These areas are known as the cradle of temples because different types of temple architecture were tried here. Even now, you can see the Nagara, Dravida and Chalukya style of temples in one place. Papanatha, Durga and Latsab temples are examples of it.

They continued with their sightseeing until it became dark.

By the time they returned, Shrimati had overcome her shyness and was able to speak to Professor Collins without any hesitation.

'Sir, you must see the temple of Kailasanatha at Ellora. It is as beautiful as the Taj Mahal. Historians believe that to build such a temple, the Rashtrakutas would have probably spent a lot, more money than to fight a war. The fact that this lovely monument was carved out of a single rock, from the top downwards, makes it even more amazing. Sir, another thing one must not miss is the statue of the enigmatically smiling Bahubali at Shravanabelagola. That too is carved out of a single boulder. And then there are the temples of Belur and Halebeedu, with which the art of sculpture reached its pinnacle.

'You need at least six months to see my country properly. You should visit us again, to comprehend the excellence my country has achieved in the creation of beauty in art and architecture.'

When they finally reached Hubli it was ten at night. While Shrimati and Collins were tired, but extremely happy, they had upset all of Shashi's plans.

The next day Professor Collins was to leave and Shrimati came to see him off at Professor Rao's house.

'Sir, I've brought a small gift for you. I hope you enjoyed yesterday's trip. To appreciate history, one need not be a historian. There was a famous mathematician in Pune who wrote about history. I have always admired his work. His name is Damodar Dharmapal Kosambi. I hope you will like the book.'

Shrimati presented a copy of *An Introduction to the Study of History*.

'Shrimati, students like you who are passionate about history must do research. If you wish, I can get you a scholarship at our university. You could either study archaeology or Asian history. You have no idea of the american system of education. It is heaven for students. You will find many facilities and excellent libraries. Students like you can do very well in that kind of atmosphere.'

Shrimati was pleasantly surprised by this offer and shyly bowed her head.

'Sir, thank you very much for your generous offer. It is very kind of you to make such an offer. But Sir, though I would like to come, I cannot accept it now. I am getting married this year.'

'Congratulations. May I ask you a personal question? Who is the lucky man?'

'He is a schoolmate of mine, Shrikant Deshpande.'

'I don't want to intrude in your personal life. But don't you feel that if you don't pursue your love of history, you will get frustrated and bored?'

'Sir, I do love history but I love Shrikant as well. I can always continue my studies later. I believe that it is not necessary to have a doctorate to gain knowledge. For me, degrees do not matter.'

'Very well, then, Shrimati. All the best for your future. I will send you photographs of our trip. Goodbye and goodluck.'

Professor Mike Collins left Hubli, thinking about her . . . Research was not merely studying. It demanded many sacrifices and hard work. Would that be possible amidst the hundred responsibilities of a family life? That too in India? He suddenly thought of his wife Jane. How had she been able to continue with her research though she was married to him? Perhaps because they never had any financial constraints. Moreover, they were co-travellers on the same road, passionate about the same subject. Dorothy was their only child. She too followed in her parents' footsteps, but disagreed with their views on marriage and family. She was living with her boyfriend Tony, who was her colleague. Although her mother had wanted them to get married, Dorothy had said a firm no.

Her argument was, 'Dad, why do we need to get married? Who says that the ultimate aim of a woman should be marriage? If marriage is only for togetherness, then aren't we together now? As soon as you get married, expectations rise and it may or may not be possible to meet all the demands. It could result in a divorce . . . I am happier this way.'

Of course, it did not mean that she had no respect or love for her parents. Only her values were different.

Professor Collins felt that Shrimati had the potential to be an excellent research scholar, but she was so different from Dorothy. She was ready to sacrifice everything for marriage.

Come to think of it, Shrimati was a better student than Dorothy, Professor Collins realized suddenly. From a very young age, Dorothy had had the advantage of a better environment and excellent training. She had toured the world with her parents and interacted with the best scholars in the subject, whereas Shrimati, who certainly possessed a sharper intellect, had never had such advantages. At this time, she was not aware of what she was getting into, but

Sudha Murty

as the years pass and the attraction between husband and wife wane and the demands of marriage increase, she would realize what she had given up was immense. Professor Collins was convinced that Shrimati should not give up her studies but then, he thought, it was her decision and her life. Perhaps what she was doing was normal in India.

Kamala noticed Shrimati growing increasingly withdrawn. She wondered whether it was because Vandana was engaged. It was natural for any girl of marriageable age to think of herself in the same situation. There was no doubt that Shrikant's recent visit had made her more restless.

Kamala was aware of her daughter's friendship with Shrikant and also of their meetings and letter-writing. But she had neither encouraged nor opposed it. She knew very well that her daughter was a sensible and mature girl. She would not do anything foolish.

Like all mothers, she also thought about Shrimati's marriage. And if by chance Kamala did not, her mother-in-law Rindakka was there to remind her about it every passing day, with a taunt. Kamala sighed, wondering whom she could discuss this matter with. Her husband was quite irresponsible. It was pointless talking to him about it.

It was a full-moon night. Everything was quiet. Kamala was sitting alone on a stone bench, deeply immersed in thoughts of her daughter.

'Avva, what are you thinking? Is it about me?' She had not seen Shrimati come up.

'Unh, yes, yes. About you and your future. You are about to complete your MA. What next?'

'Avva, that is what I wanted to discuss with you . . .'

'Is it about your marriage?' Kamala interrupted Shrimati.

Shrimati was surprised. 'How did you guess?'

'Is it with Shrikant? Did he say anything during his recent visit?'

'Yes.'

Kamala fell silent. Shrimati was perplexed since she had been sure her mother would agree at once, and with pleasure.

'Why Avva, don't you like him? Is it not correct? He is a good boy. We have known him for several years. Are you worried that he is still too young for marriage or that he is not yet working? He will speak to you when he comes next.' Shrimati's anxiety poured out in her words.

'Shrimati, I am not worried about Shrikant. I know that he is a good boy and you will live happily with him. I am only concerned about their family and our relationship with them. Shrimati, more than a mother, I have been like a friend to you. I would like to give you some advice.

'In our society, you marry not only an individual, but also his family. If I have understood them well, they will never accept you as a part of their family. They will never love you.'

'Avva, that's not true. It was probably so in your times. Those were the values of a bygone age! Things have changed now. Moreover, after the marriage I am not going to live with them! I will be with Shrikant and away from them.'

'Shrimati, some things in life have remained unaltered from time immemorial. The relations between a mother-in-law and a daughter-in-law are always strained. You have grown up as a free individual. You do not possess our patience. I want to tell you that every daughter-in-law always wants to be appreciated and loved by her in-laws. In your case, you will never get that. You will be loved only by Shrikant.'

'Why do you say that?'

'Because their expectations from a daughter-in-law are very different from Shrikant's expectations from a wife.'

Shrimati was disappointed. Over the next few days she could only think about her mother's advice. Why would her mother have said that? She was usually very silent and never said anything bad about anyone. Shrimati made up her mind to win over Rama and Gangakka.

My Shrimati,

This is the first time in five years that you have missed our letter-schedule.

What is the matter? I was expecting a detailed letter from you after my return. But you have not written at all. You may have been surprised by my proposal of marriage. After knowing that Vandana is getting married, I was worried that your people would also start searching for someone for you. If that happened, then my Shrimati would slip away from my hands and become someone else's Shrimati. In this fear, I proposed to you, though I am still a student. You are very precious to me. We have been good friends and I want that this friendship should end in marriage. In normal circumstances I would have broached this topic a couple of years after getting a job and settling down. But by then, according to our Hubli standards, you would have crossed the age of marriage. The pressure at home would have become too much for you to bear.

Shrimati, I am aware that our marriage is not going to be a simple task. The enmity between our two families is well known. The opposition will come from both the families. I understand that my mother's and your grandmother's spectrum does not stretch beyond Dharwad. But life must move forward. Today, things are different.

So, I hope we will be able to convince them and successfully cross this hurdle.

I couldn't talk to you much about my future plans as there was very little time. I am sure by now you know that I am ambitious. I don't want to be an ordinary engineer with a government job in Hubli. I want to pursue my career in the field of computers. It is not necessary for me to go abroad for it. I can do it in India, learning the latest technologies right here.

We had campus interviews recently. I have been selected by ABC Technology Ltd as a software engineer. They have offered me a good salary. Fortunately, my senior Vasudev Shenoy owns a house in Bombay. He is going abroad for three years and wants to give his house on rent. He is willing to give it to me.

I want to be in Bombay. I am in love with the city. For an outsider, it is a mechanical city with no human relationships. We have to struggle to get even ordinary things in Bombay, including basic entertainment. But still I like Bombay. It is professional, it respects hard work. The beautiful and easy life of Hubli will not be found here. Will you live with me with all these things?

I have written to my mother giving a hint about my job, my house and my desire to marry. But I have not told her your name. I am supposed to join the job in August. Whenever I am in Hubli next, I will speak to my mother about it. I have a small request. Our marriage should be very simple.

Always yours,
Shri

Gangakka too received a letter from her son. It was a special letter informing her that he had got a good job and had also found a house to live in. Reading his letter made Gangakka very happy. She thanked their family deity Lord Mylaralinga.

But at the end of the letter, there were a few lines that disturbed her. Shrikant had written, 'Avva, I am tired of hostel and hotel food. Now, I would like to get married and make a home in Bombay.'

Gangakka didn't like that. According to her, there was no hurry for him to get married. He was, no doubt, good-looking, had just finished his B.Tech., and already found a job. But he was only twenty-three years old. Twenty-three was a marriageable age for a girl, but not for a boy. If he was fed up of hostel and hotel food, he could always move back to Hubli, Gangakka thought.

She did not understand why he had to be in Bombay, an unknown place for her. She thought of her distant cousin Shyam who was a PWD engineer. He was leading a comfortable life with a car and servants in Dharwad.

Shrikant could definitely take up that kind of job. But it seemed that he wanted to be in Bombay.

Gangakka did not have the slightest inkling about Shrimati.

When a boy shows an interest in marriage, then it is unfair for a mother to keep quiet about it!

Gangakka was extremely close to her daughter Rama. They thought alike and spoke alike. The only difference was in their age. She immediately wrote to her daughter about Shrikant's decision to get married. For Rama, it was a most important occasion. She jumped with joy at the news and soon came to Hubli with her two children. Anyway, it was the summer holidays.

Mother and daughter started planning a strategy to find the kind of girl they would want for Shrikant. First of all, she had to be very obedient, extremely good-looking and from an affluent family. But they could not tell people that, they would have to put it differently.

Gangakka usually met other women of her age at the discourses on the Puranas at the temple. At these discourses, given by a pandit or the temple priest, elderly people met, exchanged ideas and experiences and got to know about each other's family matters. Such gatherings were also a broadcasting centre of news in the community. At one such meeting, Gangakka announced that she was looking for a bride for her son.

'We are looking for a good graduate girl, but not for money. If an eligible, adjusting girl comes with just a coconut, we will still be happy,' was her statement. But those who knew her, knew very well what she actually meant.

Rama's in-laws were greedy people. In order to please them Gangakka often sent them expensive gifts so that her daughter would have more prestige than the other daughters-in-law. Rama had a sister-in-law, Rajani. Now, Rama's mother-in-law was after Rama to get her horoscope matched with Shrikant's.

Rama did not like the idea at all. Telling a lie was easy for the mother and daughter. Putting on an act, Gangakka pretended as if she was very sad, and told them, 'I wish Rajani could have been my daughter-in-law! I was praying to god for that. But unfortunately the horoscopes did not match. How can we go ahead?'

A horoscope mismatch was one of the best excuses to withdraw from an unwanted proposal.

And Gangakka used this excuse as and when required.

Sheenappa, Gangakka's elder brother, was waiting for this chance. He wanted his daughter Ratna to marry Shrikant. It was customary for a boy to marry his maternal uncle's daughter in North Karnataka.

Sheenappa came with lots of gifts for his sister and Rama. He knew that if Rama was happy, she would push her mother. No one could beat Sheenappa in sweet talk. He started buttering up his sister.

'Look Gangakka, if a stranger comes as a daughter-in-law to your house, then will she take care of you in your old age? You have already suffered so much in your life. Shouldn't you be happy and get some rest at least now? Our daughter is very fond of you and she resembles Rama in most respects. She might not be as fair as Shrikant but their horoscopes have matched very well. Please do not look down upon us. We will perform the marriage in the best way. You tell me what you want . . . gold, cash . . . a house?'

It became difficult for Gangakka to resist Sheenappa's offer. She liked Ratna as a niece but did not want her to be a daughter-in-law. Ratna was arrogant, uneducated and ordinary looking.

How would Shrikant agree to marry her? It was a fact that Sheenappa had helped Gangakka in difficult times. Still, she did not want to convey her gratitude by getting into a marriage relationship.

Teaching Gangakka to talk sweetly is as unnecessary as teaching a fish to swim!

'Sheenappa, without your help I would not have survived. We all are indebted to you, and will remain, throughout our lives. Ratna was always on my mind. But

Shrikant has categorically told me that he doesn't want to marry within the family. He feels Ratna is like his own sister. I cannot go against him. I am helpless.'

Sheenappa realized that it was not Shrikant but Gangakka who did not want the alliance. Shrikant had hardly spoken to Ratna to have developed brotherly feelings. Sheenappa knew Gangakka was trying for bigger fish and Shrikant was just an excuse.

It was clear to Sheenappa that there was no use talking any further. As he was leaving, he sarcastically said, 'Okay. Marriages are made in heaven. Let us see what kind of a girl Shrikant will marry!'

At one of the Purana readings, Vandana's mother had come to know that Gangakka was searching for a daughter-in-law. Vandana's sister, Kavitha, was in her second year of BA. So their mother decided to propose a match between Kavitha and Shrikant. She knew that except for the sharp tongue and quarrelsome nature of his mother and sister, Shrikant would be the right catch.

She told Vandana, 'Shrikant was your classmate. What do you think of suggesting Kavitha for him?'

Vandana was taken aback. 'No Avva, please don't do that,' she blurted out, but did not say anything more as that would have got Shrimati into trouble.

'Why? The boy is very good and anyway they are going to stay separately in Bombay. You will also be there.'

'No Avva, whatever it is, please don't proceed. Shrikant will say no.'

'How do you say that? We will give them dowry. And Kavitha is also good-looking. Let us give them the horoscope and see. It does not mean that the marriage will take place immediately.'

Vandana's mother could not understand why Vandana was resisting so much.

All parents who had daughters suddenly started paying attention to Gangakka. They had not bothered to say even a hello to her all these years. Now they would go out of their way and talk to her and invite her to their homes. One of them was Anna Chari, the priest who gave the daily discourse at the temple. One evening after the discourse, he insisted that Rama and Gangakka come to his house for tea, though in the last twenty years, he had hardly even noticed them. Gangakka was thrilled. When she and Rama went to his house, they received royal treatment. Anna Chari's wife Champakka broached the topic in a leisurely manner as she served the varieties of food she had prepared.

'Gangakka, you never know when and how fortune smiles on a person. You are aware that the Desai family of Navalgund is very famous. They are very well-off people with plenty of land and trunks of gold in their house. They have only two daughters. The elder daughter is married to a very rich person from Bijapur. Their second daughter Indira is of marriageable age and she is very good-looking. She went up to BA but somehow didn't complete it.'

Anna Chari continued, 'What does education matter to such people? They don't need to take up a job . . . They are thinking about Shrikant, of course with my recommendation . . .'

Gangakka was overjoyed. How on earth did wealthy people like Desai think of an alliance with her family? If it came through, Shrikant would be very fortunate.

But then she remembered that they belonged to a different sect.

'Aren't they Vaishnavas?'

Normally Anna Chari would make a fuss about such things but that day, he was very liberal. 'How does it matter

Sudha Murty

Gangakka? God has two faces. One is of Lord Shiva and the other of Lord Vishnu. Both are just different names for the same god. In today's world, you should not make such differences.'

But he did not reveal that he wouldn't even drink a drop of water in a Vaishnava's house.

'What about the horoscope?' Rama raised a point.

'Oh, Gangakka! I myself have matched Shrikant's and Indira's horoscopes. They have matched excellently. Indira will bring him good luck. You should consider yourself very lucky that you have got such a proposal for Shrikant.'

Mother and daughter were thrilled! Rama started imagining Shrikant's marriage with Indira. She had heard from many people about the pomp and grandeur of their first daughter's wedding. She was sure that her status would also go up if this marriage took place.

Anna Chari was a shrewd man. He noticed the two women softening to the idea. He was just waiting for the chance. 'I will tell Desai to bring his daughter to your house this Sunday and I will also accompany them. Let us see how soon the best can happen.'

The meeting ended in good spirits.

Rama and her mother started doing up the house to impress the guests on Sunday.

Sunday finally arrived. The Desais came in a big car. Each one of them looked like royalty. Mrs Desai and Indira had worn as many ornaments as possible, to show off their status.

Rama and Gangakka took great pains to offer the best hospitality. The formalities of tea and snacks were over.

There was a disappointed look on Mrs Desai's face after seeing Gangakka's house. It was very ordinary and there was no sign of affluence. She felt that Gangakka and her daughter were too eager for this alliance, that too, just for the money.

Though Gangakka observed that the girl was a bit slow and very ordinary looking, she was tempted by her father's wealth.

Anna Chari was the only one who was talking non-stop. 'Oh, Shrikant is a very bright and simple boy and there are no two ways about it. If he applies for the IAS, he is sure to become the collector of Dharwad. He is as obedient to his mother as Shri Ramachandra. Definitely he will keep your daughter very happy.' Anna Chari did not even know that for the IAS one had to appear for an examination and not just apply.

Mrs Desai put the brakes on Anna Chari's chatter. 'Money is not at all an important factor for us. We have brought up our children in luxury and our daughter is not used to hard work. We have sufficient facilities at home. We will definitely help the boy to the best of our ability but he should keep our daughter happy.'

Gangakka diplomatically said, 'Everything depends on Shrikant's decision. Let him come and we will let you know.'

My Shri,
I received your letter and I am sorry I broke my schedule for the first time. The reasons are numerous. I wish you had stayed a little longer and we could have talked about everything in detail.

Shri, I told my mother and hesitantly, she has agreed. She has some queries, though. My mother's acceptance of our marriage is very important to me. When you come here next time, you can officially talk to my father and grandmother. Let me not create a scene now.

Are you aware of what is happening at your home? It is really scaring me. Your mother has started searching for a bride for you with great vigour, after reading about your job and all that. Every day she has an appointment at one or the other girl's house. She has no clue about us. This is the result of your not telling her. Rama is also here to help your mother. Shri, I am in no condition to bring a lot of gold and silver, to match your mother's expectations.

Regarding yourself, you know Shri, the figure of your salary is immaterial to me. The foundation of my happiness is not the digits that you earn, but the digits of your love, affection and companionship.

I am aware that life in Bombay is tough, still one percent of India's population lives there! We will be a part of that.

When you are with me,

How does it matter where we live?

Let it be a desert or a forest,

Let it be pouring rain or scorching sun,
That is heaven to me!

Shri, I have a small wish. Our marriage should be performed in the Someshwara temple in Dharwad. I hope you will understand my feelings and agree.

Waiting to be your shrimati, Shrimati

It was the beginning of June. The humidity was high, making people sweat profusely. Bustling Bombay waited impatiently for the rains to start.

It was the last day at IIT for Shrikant and his batchmates. Examinations were over, job offers and scholarships to go abroad had been received and everyone was dreaming of the future. This was probably the last time that the entire group would be together.

They had all entered this campus as teenagers and today, they were leaving as young and confident engineers, hoping to achieve fame and fortune in the outside world!

Many of them got quite emotional when they were saying goodbye to their hostel mates. But it was all part of life. Shrikant and Ravi were leaving for Hubli by the Mahalakshmi Express from VT Station.

Some of the hostellers had come to see them off.

As the train started moving, many hands waved goodbye, until the train could be seen no more.

When the train got to the outskirts of Bombay, a cool breeze started settling in. Shrikant and Ravi occupied their seats.

In the last ten days both of them had been busy packing up and sorting out last-minute paperwork. So they had not spoken much to each other. Now, they had the chance to catch up.

Sudha Murty

'Shrikant, you are well settled with a job and a house! So what is your next goal?' asked Ravi.

'Ravi, I am clear about my path. I do not want to go to the US, get a green card and settle there! When I look at young energetic directors of companies, I feel that we can stay in our own country, work hard and achieve excellence. There is no shortcut to success. Hard work and belief in oneself can take one to any position. What about you?'

'Well, you know I got a scholarship to go to the University of Pennsylvania for the winter term. So I am planning to go to the US by end December or early January. I have to go to the US and earn more money. I have two sisters to be married off . . . That reminds me, Shrikant, when are you getting married?'

'How did you guess that?'

'I didn't guess, I knew! A girl who writes to you so regularly ought to be more than a friend. I also know who she is. But Shrikant, how will you tell your people? A big battle might start.'

Ravi was aware of the family feud.

'Ravi, I know you are not only an engineer but also a good psychology student. You have found out our secret. I do not know when I chose Shrimati to be my wife, but unconsciously, I knew that she was the only girl I could marry. You tell me why.'

'Maybe because we used to tease both of you during our schooldays! When is the wedding and where is it?'

'Oh, it's going to be a simple ceremony at a temple and you must attend.'

'Certainly I will.'

Shrikant got completely immersed in his own world. He had to work and learn like the legendary Ekalavya, with single-minded devotion and perseverance. Ekalavya was a great student, he excelled in archery not with the help of a teacher, but by observing and practising with the determination to succeed. Shrikant felt that he too had to perfect his art, not giving up his ambition in life or the desire to excel.

It is one of the ironies of life that the person who is dearest to you often hurts you the most!

For two days Gangakka had not talked to her son. The silence was dreadful. The silence that comes from peace is so different compared to the silence that comes out of sorrow. She was devastated. Her only son Shrikant, on whom she had pinned so much hope, had suddenly become her enemy. The shock he had given her was like a bombshell. How could he have decided to marry that girl Shrimati?

Shrimati was hardly ten months younger to her son, ordinary looking, without money and, more than anything, her enemy's daughter! How would she face people? What would they say? They would make fun of her. And the Desais, Sheenappa and Rama's in-laws would mock her. Worse than that was the fact that her own son had gone to Rindakka's house and begged for their daughter.

Normally, a girl's parents approached the boy's people. Here it was the reverse!

Gangakka knew there was no way she could stop this marriage. Her previous excuses, that the horoscopes did not match or that they belonged to different sects, would not affect Shrikant's decision. Gangakka was so upset that she was not able to eat. She sobbed continuously. She had experienced this kind of sorrow for the first time after her husband's death.

Shrikant tried very hard to console her. 'Avva, you have a wrong impression about Shrimati. She is a very nice, kind and bright girl. She will look after you very well. Please do not depend upon dowry. However much money you want, I will give you once I start earning. If you care for my happiness, please accept Shrimati as your daughter-in-law. I will be unhappy marrying anyone else.'

'She is our enemy's daughter!'

'Avva, I am not marrying her grandmother. Have you ever found Shrimati or her mother fighting with you? Not even once probably. Then why this objection?'

'They belong to the Vaishnava community.'

'Avva, think of the outside world. You have not thought beyond Hubli–Dharwad. People marry from different countries. Ours would only be different sects of the same community, after all. Our languages, our food habits are all the same.'

But Gangakka was not willing to listen to anything.

Shrikant got frustrated and went out.

Gangakka was sleeping on a mat on the floor. She looked like she was on strike. Rama came in. She was equally furious with her brother. Though she belonged to the younger generation, she was worse than Gangakka in her old-fashioned views. She even outdid her mother when it came to planning and scheming.

As soon as Gangakka met her daughter, both of them broke down in each other's arms. Rama tried to comfort her mother.

'Avva, don't cry and waste your energy. Your tears will not change his decision. If he has decided to marry her, then let us think of the other things. First of all, tell everybody that the girl is intelligent and smart, and that we have agreed to this marriage. Don't ever tell them the real reason. Second, I know that you have kept money and some gold for his marriage. You need not give them to his wife. Third he has told you that he will look after you. You need not go and stay with him. Just tell him to send money every month.' At these words, Gangakka was a little consoled.

On the other side of the compound, in Shrimati's house, her father and grandmother were also strongly opposed to the alliance. They felt there was nothing special about Shrikant. He had just got a job, was not yet properly settled and their Shrimati was any day more intelligent than him. Moreover, he was their enemy's son.

Despite these misgivings, Shrimati's marriage to Shrikant took place on a rainy day in Shravan at the Someshwara temple in Atthikolla. Atthikolla was full of wild flowers and there was much greenery around. Among the very few people who attended the marriage, most of them were their classmates.

Normally, wedding garlands are made of jasmine, rajanigandha or sevanthige. But for this wedding, the garlands were made of bakula flowers.

Shrimati looked her usual self, only, she was wearing a new cotton saree, green glass bangles and lots of bakula strings in her plait. She had the same enchanting smile that had captivated Shrikant, and prevented him from seeing any other girl.

After the simple wedding ceremony was over, Ravi Patil shook hands with Shrikant and said, 'Shrimati, today you are officially Shrimati Shrikant Deshpande. Our prophecy has come true.'

Shrimati smiled, with a blush.

As expected, Shrimati was made to feel unwelcome in Gangakka's house. Still, she wanted to win over her mother-in-law. So she tried to help her in the kitchen. But Gangakka made it clear that the kitchen was her domain and she didn't want Shrimati to enter it.

She would say, 'You have just married. You do not know our customs. So please don't bother about cooking.'

Within a week, Shrimati got bored. When she went to her house, her grandmother would ask her innumerable questions, 'Shrimati, what did your mother-in-law give you in marriage? I saw her in a saree shop the other day. Did she get you a saree?'

Shrimati could not answer any of her queries.

When Shrikant was there, Gangakka would be cordial but when he went out she would show her true colours by saying hurtful things to Shrimati.

'I really don't understand your customs. You call Shrikant by his first name and that too in a short form. We believe that if you address your husband by his name, you shorten his lifespan. Your mother should have taught you all these manners. There is a saying, *The quality of the saree depends on its thread and the nature of a daughter depends on her mother's.*'

In the previous generations, when the husband was usually older than the wife, he would not be addressed by name. But Shrikant was only ten months older than Shrimati. Besides, they had grown up together. So it was hard for Shrimati to change. Whenever she tried, Shrikant would not allow it, saying, 'Shrimati, get out of that old custom! When I can call you by your first name, you should also be able to do the same. First, we were good friends and now, I have become your husband. That's all.'

Shrikant would also tease her saying that he knew she would some day become his wife and that is why he wanted her to call him Shri.

Shrimati would become very dejected whenever Gangakka hurt her like this. Her mother was such a gentle, docile person, she would never have taught her daughter wrong things or given her bad advice. Shrimati felt very helpless when her mother was criticized by Gangakka, but she said nothing.

Ten days after the marriage, Shrikant and his Shrimati came to Bombay. It was the month of August. The monsoon had set in and it was pouring in Bombay. Bombay rains are so different from the rains in Dharwad. The continuous rain would disrupt local life, but the disciplined citizens of Bombay never complained.

Shrimati was shocked to see her small single-bedroom apartment at Bandra.

It was probably smaller than a room in their Hubli house. There was no question of a garden or a bakula tree in a place like Bombay.

'Shri, why should we pay a thousand rupees rent for such a small house?'

Shrikant laughed at her innocence.

'Shrimati, it is very difficult to get an apartment in Bandra without paying an advance. Be happy about this house. It is only thanks to Vasudev that we got it.'

'Shri, what's so great about Bandra?'

'Shrimati, Bandra is a very expensive area. It is very well connected. Gradually, you will understand all that.'

Shrikant reported for work, as a software engineer, on the appointed day. He was on probation for six months. Among the many people who joined the company that day, he was the only person who was married. Though it seemed a little odd, Shrikant was never embarrassed about it.

Shrimati was left alone at home. She would keep remembering her mother, her Hubli house, and the quiet atmosphere of their hometown. All these memories would make her homesick. Her eyes would well up with tears. Kamala had not shed a single tear at her daughter's marriage. She had held it in with sheer willpower.

Now Shrimati started seeing her mother in a new light. At least for her, life was fun with a loving husband, a new city, new experiences . . . But for her mother? Her only friend was Shrimati! How is she managing without me, Shrimati wondered. This was the first time in twenty-two years that Shrimati was away from her mother.

She also remembered Gangakka's frequent taunts.

'Shrimati, the colour of the saree your mother has given me is not good.'

'Avva, for that price, it would have been the best one,' Rama would add.

'How much money did your parents spend for the marriage?'

Shrimati did not know what to answer, but Rama would support her mother saying, 'It would have definitely been less than what the Desais would spend on one day of Diwali.'

Shrimati was so soft-spoken and well-behaved that it was difficult for her to answer back. Besides, she had just got married. She did not want to create any problems for anyone.

Sudha Murty

After her marriage Vandana too shifted to Bombay. But she lived far away, near the Arland Church at Malad, another suburb of Bombay.

Unlike Hubli, in spite of being in the same city, it was not easy to meet her often.

Shrimati found it difficult to confide in Vandana about her problems because Vandana's in-laws were very affectionate people.

When Shrimati went to their house, she saw Vandana's mother-in-law giving her a saree for the Gowri festival. Though it was not an expensive one, it was a token of affection!

Whenever something was to be given to her daughter-in-law, Gangakka on the other hand would say, 'Oh that is not our custom' or 'You are too modern, so I have not given you anything.'

Irrespective of all this, life was very happy for Shrimati because of Shrikant. They were young, they were starting a new home and Gangakka was not present physically!

Soon, Shrimati started getting used to Bombay. She took up cooking for the first time in her life. Shrikant was a hard working person and a dutiful husband. Right at the beginning of the month he would hand over his entire salary to her. He had told her, 'Shrimati, my mother has suffered a lot. She has sacrificed so much for my education. So, every month, you must send her thousand rupees. Then with the rest, you manage the house. I won't ask you anything.'

She did not have any expensive habits, so Shrikant's salary was more than enough for her. Without fail, she would send thousand rupees to her mother-in-law.

Shrikant too had simple tastes. His only luxury was technical books which he would buy because they were essential for his work. Shrimati knew about it and would keep some money aside. On his modest salary they had enough for their needs, but not for luxuries. Some weekends, Shrimati and Shrikant would visit nearby tourist sites like the Elephanta Caves, Bhaja, Karla and other places of interest. Shrikant was not really interested in these historical places but for Shrimati's sake he would go.

Six months after their wedding Shrimati got a letter from Professor Collins in reply to the wedding invitation she had sent him.

He wrote that he had been a visiting professor in South America for six months. As a wedding gift he sent her a set of Roman and Greek history books. This was the best gift Shrimati had received.

Shrikant was confirmed as a permanent employee within three months of his training instead of the usual six months, since his performance had been very good. As a result he became busier by the day. His company, which was of a moderate size, was growing rapidly and Shrikant started growing with the company. Within a year's time, everyone had heard about him. His general manager, Mr Vishwas Kelkar, had taken a great liking to Shrikant because of his hardworking nature. He would work even on Sundays. He never uttered the words, 'Sorry, I cannot do it.'

Sometimes, Shrikant would work the entire night. At such times he would ask Shrimati to carry dinner to the office for him. Bombay being a safe place, Shrimati would take a local train, give him his dinner and come back. Initially, she would wonder how people travelled in such crowded trains. But now, she was one of them.

It was the custom for a newly-wed couple to go to the parents' place for the first Diwali after marriage. Shrikant and Shrimati were supposed to go to Hubli, but because of some urgent assignment, Shrikant could not go and Shrimati had to go alone. She had made it a point to take gifts for Gangakka and Rama. Even after all these months, the treatment she received from them was no different.

The first year of Shrikant and Shrimati's marriage flew by and Shrimati had become a Bombayite. The charm of discovering Bombay had worn off and she had started feeling a little lonely. She seriously began to think of continuing her studies and Shrikant welcomed the idea whole-heartedly. At times, Shrikant would feel bad that his intelligent wife was whiling away her time in Bombay. So, he encouraged her to study further. But a letter from Gangakka jeopardized everything.

Gangakka had written, 'For your studies, I had taken a loan of one lakh rupees. One part of that money I took from your uncle Sheenappa and the other from my cousin Shyam. Now Sheenappa's daughter Ratna is getting married and Shyam is building another house. Both of them have asked for the money back, at the earliest. Maybe you can send ten instalments of ten thousand rupees. They are nice people and have not asked for any interest. Maybe Sheenappa is asking for the money because he is upset that you did not marry his daughter, I do not know. However, I feel that it is your duty to return the money now . . .'

The real reason for Gangakka's letter was something entirely different. Gangakka was extremely miserable that her daughter-in-law was happy. She could see the happiness when Shrimati had come to Hubli for Diwali.

She was envious of Shrimati. All these days, Shrikant was solely her property. She could not bear the fact that now he also belonged to Shrimati. Gangakka's happiness was inversely proportional to Shrimati's.

As Shrimati was physically far away from her, Gangakka had to find other ways to trouble her. Though Shrimati invited Gangakka to Bombay many times, she refused to go. She said she would get bored there. Besides, it was Shrimati's house, after all.

Bombay was too far for Rama to visit them often, but she did spend a lot of time with her mother.

It was Rama's idea to ask Shrikant for the money. 'Let us ask Shrikant for a huge sum. That will make Shrimati struggle.'

'But on what pretext can I ask?'

'Tell him that you had taken a loan for his education.'

They knew that Shrikant would be hurt in the process, but they felt that he deserved it because he had married Shrimati.

Shrimati was scared when she read that letter. How on earth would they get a lakh of rupees? Neither did they have so much money nor could her parents afford to lend it. Shrikant was worried too. He could not ask for a loan from his company in the second year itself. After he had been made permanent, his salary had increased, but he also had to set up a new house, and buy everything from scratch.

Shrimati suddenly found a solution.

'Shri, can I get a job?'

'Yes, you may get one, but not in any history department, where you will be paid very little.'

'Don't worry, Shri, I will take up any job anywhere for a year and save money.'

'But you wanted to study, Shrimati!'

'The day we send the last instalment, I will stop working and pursue my studies. It doesn't matter if I am late by a year. Can you please find a job for me?'

'Shrimati, you can get an administrative job, but it is not really meant for people like you. You are a different kind of person, your talents are in a totally different area. More than that, why should you repay my loan?'

Shrimati smiled and answered, 'When you are mine, your loan is also mine. It comes as a package. I cannot say I want only my husband. His joys and difficulties are also acceptable to me.'

Shrikant was too moved to speak.

He actually believed that his mother had taken that huge loan. He never suspected any foul play on her part. He trusted his mother and strongly believed that she would never do him any wrong.

He was also hurt that Shrimati had to work for more than a year for his sake and postpone her Ph.D. He was aware that it was unfair to her.

With the help of Mr Kelkar, Shrimati got a job with a small import–export company in the Fort area of downtown Bombay. The salary was good but the job was mechanical. Shrimati had to leave home at seven in the morning and returned at seven in the night. With some hesitation, Shrimati joined the company. Her Parsi boss, Mr Farooq Modi, was a decent man. He was a good friend of Mr Kelkar. Both of them were members of the same club on Charni Road. There was a predominance of women in the office as Mr Modi firmly believed that women worked harder than men.

Shrimati soon became very popular in the office because of her non-interfering nature and her habit of working hard. She did not enjoy the job much since it was monotonous, but she did enjoy the company of all her colleagues. They came from different parts of Bombay. Shrimati became friendly with three of them—Nalini Bapat, Marukh and Shanta Iyer. She often went shopping with them but she wouldn't spend a rupee on anything. Her main goal was to save as much as she could.

All the money Nalini earned, she spent on gold ornaments. Marukh would spend her's on clothes. Shanta had a big responsibility, as she looked after a huge family.

Every month, Shrimati would send Gangakka her entire salary along with some savings from Shrikant's salary.

Sudha Murty

When Gangakka received the first instalment, her joy knew no bounds. She had not expected her obedient son and sincere daughter-in-law to take her demand so seriously. They said they would send her the money in ten instalments. She regretted not telling them that the amount was two lakhs instead of one!

Now that she had excess money in her hands, Gangakka decided to use this bonus amount to buy ornaments for Rama. Rama was thrilled. Neither she nor her mother realized that this money was at the cost of the bright young Shrimati's future.

After fifteen months, Shrimati decided to resign. All her friends felt that she was being impractical. Nalini, in particular, told her, 'Shrimati, you must always earn your own money, irrespective of your husband's income. His money can never be yours. A day could come when he may say that this is my money and I will spend it the way I want and suppose you want to spend something, you will be at his mercy.'

Shanta advised her, 'Shrimati, be practical. You don't have work at home. Extra earning is always a great incentive. You never know how the days are ahead. This is a good company, try to continue as long as possible.'

Shrimati knew that it was their affection for her that made them advise her. In an impersonal place like Bombay, no one advised anyone on personal matters. Shrimati said to them, 'Thank you for your sincere advice. For me, there is no difference between Shrikant's money and my money. I am not in the habit of spending money on myself. Besides, if I did want to, he would never object. Actually, I want to register for my Ph.D in history.'

Mr Modi, her boss, tried to persuade her, 'Shrimati, why do you want to resign? If you want, I will raise your salary. You are a good worker. I don't want to lose you.'

Shrimati politely declined his offer. When she came home that day, she was so relieved and happy. With the last instalment, Shrikant wrote a note to his mother, thanking her for providing him with a good education, in spite of all the difficulties. He did not forget to mention that it was only because of Shrimati's hard work that he had been able to send the money.

Gangakka was furious when she read his letter. 'What is so great about Shrimati? She did not bring any dowry, so she has repaid his loan, that's all.'

Sudha Murty

One evening, Shrikant told Shrimati, 'Don't cook at home today. We will go out to eat.'

'No Shri, it will be expensive,' Shrimati replied.

'It's all right. One day we can afford to eat outside.'

'Are you getting a pay rise?'

'Of course. I am going to be a manager now.'

'Oh! Within two and a half years?' she asked with surprise and happiness.

'Don't go by the number of years. I have probably worked as much as a normal person would in five years. My salary has increased but the cost of living also has gone up. So we should send more money to my mother. At least now she can get something for Rama without asking me. Let her be economically independent.'

Shrimati became silent for a moment, before agreeing to what Shrikant said.

She did not want to curb Shri's happiness by speaking what was on her mind. Shrimati remembered the ingratitude of Gangakka who hadn't said a single word to her about the loan, knowing very well about her contribution.

This was the first time the two of them were having dinner outside home. Both of them walked up to Dhanaraj Restaurant in Bandra.

While Shrimati was looking at the menu card, Shrikant warned her playfully, 'At least today don't look at the price, Shrimati!'

Shrimati put the menu card aside and asked, 'Shri, what are your responsibilities in the new job?'

'I may have to travel more. A group will report to me. My boss Mr Kelkar has great confidence in me and he expects that I should work with total concentration. The salary hike comes with more responsibility, of course.'

'Hey, Shri, when you talk about concentration I am reminded of one of the stories . . .'

'Hope it is not the usual long historical one!' Shrikant interrupted.

'Yes, it is, but you must listen.'

'I don't have much choice when I am married to a historian,' Shrikant joked and got ready to listen to her.

'Long ago, there was a young sage who wanted to write a commentary on the Dharmashastra. He was so focused in his work that he had forgotten about the outside world. His poor mother used to look after him and when she realized that she was getting older, she went to the next village and chose a bride for him. As an obedient son should, he went there and got married. Even after his marriage, this sage remained busy in studying and writing, not bothering about his young wife.'

'That sounds a bit unusual, not bothering about a wife!' Shrikant made fun of the story.

'No, Shri, it can happen when one is totally focused. When the sage's mother died, the young bride did not wait for her husband but came on her own to his house. She understood the situation. She used to work outside and get money, cook for her husband and look after him like a mother. This man continued his work. Time passed by and one night, after he had completed the last line of the book, he noticed an old woman sleeping on the floor. He recognized her face but could not remember who she was. He woke her up and asked, "Lady, who are you? When did you come here?" She replied politely that she was his wife and explained that she had been with him for the last forty years, ever since his mother had died.

'The sage was wonderstruck. He could not believe that this woman had done so much for him. He asked her with great respect, "What is your name?"

'"My name is Bhamati."

'Then he wrote on the first page of the text, "Bhamati". Till date, the book *Bhamati* is referred to by many Sanskrit scholars. Bhamati signifies all those women who sacrifice their youth for the betterment of their husbands. Nobody remembers that sage's name but Bhamati stands out.'

Shrikant was listening very carefully.

'Shri, whose sacrifice do you find more praiseworthy?'

Shrikant thought for a minute and said, 'Of course, both of them, but I feel the single-minded perseverance of the sage, without getting distracted by the worldly pleasures, is praiseworthy.'

'I don't agree with you, Shri. I think the sacrifice made by Bhamati is unparalleled. She spent her entire youth without asking anything or complaining. His work would not have been completed but for her. More than that, I like something else.'

'What is that?'

'The fact that the husband recognized his wife's sacrifice and named the book after her. That is what appeals to me more.'

'Oh Shrimati, in today's society it is very difficult to find women like Bhamati. They have changed so much.'

It was three years since they were married and now, Shrimati was keen to enroll for her Ph.D. But around that time, Shrikant was posted to Delhi.

Shrimati was sad. She did not want to part with Shrikant or the Ph.D. Shrikant reasoned, 'Either I reject my offer to go to Delhi or you stay alone in Bombay to do your Ph.D. If I go to Delhi, I can come here only once a month.'

'No Shri, neither option is acceptable. I don't want you to forgo your promotion by rejecting this offer, nor do I want to stay alone. We will stay in Delhi for one year and I will take up my studies next year. Anyway north India has a lot of historical places that I can visit.'

Shrimati had started compromising.

'Shrimati, there is one more way. We can ask my mother to come and stay with you.'

Though she did not say it, Shrimati knew very well that Gangakka wouldn't agree.

In the meantime, Gangakka's life had also changed. There was a phone at home now. When Shrikant called her up to ask her about coming to Bombay to stay with Shrimati, Gangakka said, 'I wish I could come and help your wife. She is just like a daughter to me. But I am planning to go on a pilgrimage for two months. Sheenappa's wife is unwell. He has helped me when I was alone and you were still a child. So I have to help them now. Rama's children may also come here to study. You tell me what I should do. I will listen to you.'

So, Gangakka's coming to Bombay was ruled out.

Shrimati left for Delhi with Shrikant. For a person like her, neither very ambitious nor very courageous, such situations meant that her own priorities were always pushed to the lowest rung.

Spending a year in the historic city of Delhi did not prove to be very difficult for Shrimati. It was a new place and she made new friends, so she did not get bored.

'Shrikant, after we go back from Delhi, the lease period of our present house will be over. Where can we take up a new house? Can we afford to buy one?'

Sudha Murty

'Shrimati, don't worry. Now I can ask for a housing loan from my company.'

'In that case, let's buy a house in Versova, one that faces the sea.'

'Why there, Shrimati? It is so far.'

'Somehow, I am fascinated by the sea. I can sit in front of the water for any number of hours. I can view my dreams in the rise and fall of the waves.'

'Oh Shrimati, please don't get so poetic and dreamy. I cannot understand you. But one thing is certain, I cannot stay in Versova.'

'Shri, without dreams life is nothing. Don't you dream of becoming the director of a company?'

'Come on. That is a practical dream.'

'Okay. Where shall we buy the house?'

'Let us see, somewhere in Santa Cruz or Bandra, maybe.'

Many unexpected things happen in life, and Shrikant's life was not an exception. His career had gone very well, his boss was extremely happy with his performance in Delhi and now he was being promoted as a project manager and sent to Los Angeles, USA.

Shrikant had been to the US a few times before but this time, he was going to stay there for three years.

Mr Kelkar had assured him that the company would take care of his wife's travel as well as their living expenses for three years.

Shrimati was thrilled. She took loads of presents from Delhi for her parents, Rama and her children and Gangakka, before leaving for the US.

With the sudden affluence, Gangakka could afford to make some changes around her. She got the house repaired and did it up with modern interiors. She acquired several new household appliances. She had more time to gossip now. But her feelings towards Shrimati had not changed, even after five years of her marriage to Shrikant. She had never shown any affection towards Shrimati. Though there was a phone at home, she never called her. Shrimati tried her level best but failed miserably to win her mother-in-law's confidence. Gangakka no longer taunted her about dowry. Now it was about not having children.

'Shrimati, wasn't Sharada your classmate? It seems she delivered her third child last week. I had gone to Vandana's son's birthday and she told me. Her son is very good-looking.'

Rama poured fuel on the conversation, 'Remember Indira, Desai's daughter whom Anna Chari had proposed for Shrikant? She gave birth to twin boys. Her in-laws are indeed very lucky.'

Shrimati felt suffocated in this atmosphere but did not have any answer to their comments. Many a times she would feel like telling them to advise their son instead. But her shyness wouldn't allow her.

Shrimati had once said to Shrikant, 'Shri, we have been married for five years now. All our friends are already parents. I feel like having a child now.'

But Shrikant was very adamant regarding them having children.

'So what, Shrimati? We got married at an early age because our circumstances were different. I am hardly twenty-eight years old. Let us first settle down. Many of our classmates are still not married. Look at Ravi, Anthony . . . Let's not be in a hurry to have a baby.'

How could she tell Gangakka all this?

Kamala was very happy and thanked god that her son-in-law was doing very well and her daughter was happy, unlike herself. Shrimati's father Shrikantrao, on the other hand, boasted saying that though Shrikant wasn't the proper match, still they got their daughter married to him. He claimed that Shrikant's prosperity was because of his daughter's horoscope.

At times Kamala did feel bad that Shrimati did not have any children yet, but she was not like Gangakka, to talk directly about it. She was aware that Shrimati was very sensitive. So she indirectly told her daughter that it was the right time to have children. Shrimati replied, 'Avva, I am aware of it but for this, Shrikant should agree.'

Gangakka was very happy that her son was doing well but at the same time, she was extremely unhappy that Shrimati too was going abroad. So when Shrimati would visit Hubli, Gangakka would find some reason to go out of station and wouldn't return until Shrimati had left. She just couldn't stand Shrimati's presence. If at all Gangakka was present, Shrimati was not allowed to work in the kitchen because Gangakka never liked Vaishnava food. The situation in Shrimati's mother's place was no different. Her grandmother found fault with her and said Shrimati had taken her mother-in-law's side and become a Smartha.

But the real reason for Shrimati's unhappiness was the lack of love and affection from Gangakka and Rama. No matter what she did, it was wrong in their eyes. Shrimati was upset because somewhere within herself she felt she had failed. She acutely felt that she was an unwanted member in Shrikant's family. And yet, she hoped that they would love her and accept her some day.

She knew love and affection cannot be taught or purchased with money. The sincere feeling of fondness should come from within the heart. It doesn't matter if the person has wealth, intelligence or beauty. In her case, though it was a futile exercise, still she was hopeful that some day things would change. Sometimes, when she was alone in her mother's place, many things would come to her mind.

Professor Rao and his wife knew Shrimati very well and they had been very keen that Shrimati should marry their elder son who was a doctor in the US. But Shrimati had declined that proposal politely because of her commitment to Shrikant. Perhaps if she had married someone whose parents liked her, things would have been different. Of course, she never regretted marrying Shrikant. His love and affection was complete and he was loyal to her. But to live in society, one required a lot of support from the family too! Even after so many years she never felt at home in Gangakka's house. She was still an outsider. But how could she explain all this to her mother or to Shri?

Vandana's mother was nice to her but because Shrikant was doing so well and Shrimati was very well-off now, she would taunt her in a different way.

'Oh Shrimati, we spent so much for Vandana's wedding, but you are very lucky. Even without spending a paisa from your father's pocket, you have caught hold of a nice guy. I hope Kavitha will learn a little bit from you.'

It was true that Vandana's husband was not as smart as Shrikant and had not gone ahead in his career. But Shrikant was not only intelligent, he was also hard-working. That's why he was so successful.

Shrimati went to meet Sharada at her in-laws' place. Theirs was a joint family. There was hardly any privacy. Sharada was busy with all the household chores, but she was very happy to receive her old friend. Unfortunately they hardly got any time to talk.

'Shrimati, do you remember how you used to insist that I should complete my BA. At times I feel what is its use now? I have not touched a book ever since I finished the BA exams. But tell me, Shrimati, you must be having lots of friends in Bombay?'

'No, Shari, I don't. Actually, I have very few friends now. We all grew up together without expecting anything from each other. Today things are different.' Then changing the topic, Shrimati asked her friend, 'Shari, why did you have a third child in this day and age?'

This reminded Shrimati of the conversation she had had with Shrikant, how he had proposed to her and said that they could not afford a third child whom she had declared she would call Siddhartha Gautama.

'It was my mother-in-law, she wanted a male child. It is very necessary for our business-oriented family. And as you know, my first two were daughters.'

'Then you must have prayed a lot to Bhandiwad Maruti and offered pedas!' Shrimati said with a laugh.

Shrimati was thrilled that she was going to the US. She had been in touch with Professor Collins through letters but had not met him. This was a good opportunity for her to go to Chicago and meet him and his daughter Dorothy.

Shrikant, now one of the seniormost in his company, was happy that he could understand the global market and explore global business.

He knew that if he worked harder and proved himself, he would be made a vice-president in a couple of years. Right now, he was posted as head of the American operations.

Shrikant had plenty of responsibilities. His boss Mr Kelkar was pinning all his hopes on Shrikant, so Shrikant made it very clear to Shrimati that life in America would be hectic and she was not to expect anything from him. He would like her to be on her own, he said.

When the Deshpandes arrived in Los Angeles, they were given a well-furnished two-bedroom apartment by the company. After a year, they could consider moving to another place. For Shrimati, everything was new and fascinating . . . the market, the roads, the people, everything. And she was keen to learn about all those new things. Since the public transport system in Los Angeles, or LA as it is popularly called, was not good, Shrimati and Shrikant had to learn driving. They purchased two second-hand cars, an absolute necessity, rather than a luxury.

After they had settled down and Shrimati felt more confident about travelling on her own, she went to Chicago to meet Professor Collins. There she also met Dorothy. Dorothy had finished her Ph.D and was working in the University. Professor Collins's home was full of books, journals, research papers and documents on history. The atmosphere in their home, the conversation, the fascinating work they did, was truly a treat for Shrimati.

As Dorothy was travelling to Europe, she suggested that Shrimati should join her. The entire tour would take three months.

Shrikant was most encouraging. He wanted his wife to be bold and independent. So Shrimati went on the tour and thoroughly enjoyed herself.

One year went by very quickly. Shrimati was beginning to feel quite at home in LA. But a sudden phone call upset everything.

They got the sad news that Vishwas Kelkar had died of a heart attack and Shrikant was required to report to the India office immediately.

Shrikant left Shrimati to wind up everything and returned to India alone. It would take her a couple of months to complete all the formalities. He knew she was capable of handling them on her own.

On his way back to India, Shrikant kept thinking about Mr Kelkar and his sudden demise. He had been a man of clean habits, always on his toes, working relentlessly all the time. He had suffered from a gastric ulcer, caused, as he used to say, by tension. He would dismiss it humorously as an 'executive disease'.

What was the cause of the stress? There had been rumours that Vishwas was not happy at home and had some marital problems. Did that affect his health and cause the heart attack?

Shrikant could not help wondering why he had been called back when there were so many people more senior to him in the Bombay office. Was there something special awaiting him?

Yes. There was. The board of directors felt that he would be the right person to succeed Mr Kelkar.

Though he had spent only six years with the company, they gave him the general manager's post, on probation for six months. Depending on his performance, he would be confirmed. Shrikant was extremely happy.

The next day he went to the general manager's office and saw the empty chair. For a minute he was scared, thinking of the tension the person who occupied that chair had to undergo. The price, for an ambitious person, is heavy. He remembered Vishwas's words and repeated them to himself again. 'The goddess of success does not knock on your door twice. Every opportunity should be completely utilized. A smart person is one who converts every failure into success. Success does not always mean knowledge. There are many factors that make a person successful. Hard work, courage to take risks, and also the ability to make people realize that you work hard. The person who works from nine to five will never become successful. Only he who thinks about the company all the time and focuses on his work, can be successful.'

Now, all that Shrikant had to do was concentrate and focus on his work. He had got his opportunity and he had to succeed. He would show his seniors that he was indispensable. That was not difficult for him.

Sudha Murty

Shrimati arrived in India three months after Shrikant's return. Shrikant went to the airport to receive her.

He was overjoyed to see her after such a long time. When they came out, Shrimati saw a new car and a driver waiting for them.

Shrimati was surprised, 'Hey, Shri, what's this?'

'Shrimati, the company has given me Vishwas's position,' Shrikant told her beaming with happiness. 'They have confirmed me as general manager after just three months instead of six.'

'Congratulations! But why didn't you inform me before?'

'I wanted to give you a surprise. Are you happy?'

'Shri, I have always been a part of your life. Your achievements have always been mine.'

Shrimati noticed the car was taking a different route.

'Shri, where are we going?'

'I have purchased a new three-bedroom flat near Bandstand in Bandra, facing the sea. You will love it.'

Shrimati looked worried.

'Shri, how much money have you borrowed for that? We will have to work throughout our life to repay that loan, is it?'

'Shrimati, are you mad. I am general manager now. I have a different status. The company has given me an interest-free loan.'

'What is the name of our apartment?'

'Sea Waves.'

'Shri, how did you manage these things all by yourself?'

'When I managed to get the first-ranker Shrimati, this is nothing.'

'Oh, come on, Shri, tell me seriously.'

'Success is never accidental. One has to plan for it.'

When they reached the apartment, Shrimati was amazed. The place was way beyond her imagination. It was a very posh and well-furnished house, befitting Shrikant's new position. There were three balconies and from every balcony she had a view of the sea.

With the new designation, life had changed enormously for Shrikant, but not for Shrimati. He had become extremely busy and was touring a lot. He travelled twenty to twenty-five days a month. His life only revolved around his company, nothing else.

One monsoon evening Shrimati was sitting in the balcony, staring at the road. The rain was splashing on to the balcony and she was getting wet. But she continued sitting there, with no inclination to get up. That morning she had noticed a few grey hairs on her head. Suddenly she began to feel age was catching up with her.

Everything had worked out well for them, financially at least. But they still didn't have any children.

The previous evening, Vandana had come to visit Shrimati with her two children. Vandana still stayed in Malad but in a two-bedroom apartment. Once in a while they would meet. The years of friendship between the two women allowed them to discuss even intimate, personal matters with each other.

'Shrimati, I hope you don't mind me asking this question, but don't you get bored without children?'

'Of course I get bored. I have gone to a gynaecologist and she says everything is normal.'

'No, you should go to a specialist. You don't have any shortage of money. You better go to Hinduja Hospital at Mahim. There is a very well-known doctor there called Dr Phadke. Don't go alone. Take Shrikant with you. But don't delay it any further.'

Vandana's advice was what Shrimati had been thinking about as she sat on the balcony that night.

As usual, Shrikant came home at nine o'clock in the night. After his dinner, he quickly settled down to read the *Financial Express*. Shrimati came and sat next to him on the sofa and broached the topic.

'Shri, I am getting bored at home.'

Without even looking at her, Shrikant said, 'I have told you several times to register for a Ph.D but you don't seem to be bothered at all.'

'No, Shri, I want something more important than that.'

'Then take computer classes. That will help you a lot and once you start surfing, you wouldn't even know how time flies.'

Shrimati got really upset. How is it that he didn't even think of children?

'Shri, the computer is not everything in life. If you want me to learn about computers, then you study a little bit about my subject. Moreover, I am not interested in getting a degree for any financial gain. I obey what my heart tells me.'

Shrikant found her words strange. 'Shrimati, in real life you should always decide with your head, not with your heart. If you don't do that, it's disastrous.'

'That is your way of thinking, Shri. I need not learn computers because there is an expert at home. I don't have any inclination for it. Just because you have a rope at home do you go and buy a buffalo for that? Education and marriage are the two things where you have to obey your heart. In the West, you can change your marriage partner and your subject of education whenever you want, but not in our rigid society . . .'

Shrikant stopped her speech by taking hold of her hands.

'Now, what do you want? Tell me straight,' he said.

'Shri, let us go to some specialist . . .'

'Why, what's wrong with you? Are you unwell?' Shrikant was perturbed.

'No, Shri, I am perfectly all right, but don't you think we should have children now? We are well settled financially. Both of us are over thirty, and thirty is late for a woman.'

Shrikant was silent for a minute. Then he said, 'Okay. Make an appointment and we will go.'

The following week they met Dr Phadke. Dr Phadke was a senior doctor with more than fifty years of experience. He had seen many childless couples and could understand their anxiety.

Shrikant did the talking. He asked questions about why they were unable to have children. Was there anything wrong? Was the defect in him or in Shrimati? Could it be corrected?

Dr Phadke smiled.

'Well, Mr Deshpande, where are you working?'

Shrikant replied confidently, 'I am the general manager of a software company.'

'The human body is not a computer. Many a times we do not know why things happen in a particular way. We can give the probable reason but not the exact one. We can also prescribe a medicine that may possibly rectify the problem, but each human body reacts differently to the same medicine. So, it is not easy to give definite answers. However, I would like you both to undergo certain tests and get back to me with the results.'

The whole of the following week, Shrikant and Shrimati spent taking all the tests that were advised by the doctor. Shrikant showed no emotion or anxiety during the tests whereas Shrimati underwent a turbulence of emotions. She prayed for good results.

When they met Dr Phadke the next time, they could not make out what was on the doctor's mind by looking at his face.

After going through all the reports, Dr Phadke smiled and said, 'Mr and Mrs Deshpande, both of you are educated and intelligent. So, it should be easy for you to understand this. Neither of you has any problem. But in order to have children, either the field or the seed must be very potent. If both are potent then it is very easy. But in your case, both have ordinary potency. In medical terms we call this "sub-fertile". That does not mean that you cannot have children at all. It might perhaps take longer for you to conceive.'

Shrimati's eyes filled with tears of disappointment. But she took hold of herself and asked, 'Doctor, you must have seen many cases such as ours. How long could it take for people like us to have children?'

'Shrimati, other people's experience is irrelevant for you. It depends upon the individual body. For some people it may take ten years and for others maybe only five. You should not lose heart.'

Shrimati was holding back her tears until she reached home. As soon as they reached home, she burst into tears.

Wouldn't Ashoka, Vikramaditya, Siddhartha Gautama, about whom they had talked so much before marriage, be born in their family? Would there not be any heir to Shrikant's and her intelligence? Would their family end there? Shrimati felt utterly hopeless and helpless. The gates of her dam of sorrows broke open and tears gushed out as floods.

All the children she had dreamt of would remain only dreams. She remembered Gangakka referring to her as a barren woman. How could she convince the uneducated, unsympathetic Gangakka that she was not to be blamed, but neither was Shrikant. She continued sobbing.

Shrikant came and put his arms around her. His touch only increased her sorrow. It was getting dark. Shrimati had not yet put the lights on. She felt that her life was full of darkness now.

Shrikant consoled her. 'Come on, Shrimati, take it easy. This is not the end of our lives. I don't believe in such things. If we do not have children then we will have only one worry. On the contrary if we have children and if they don't come up well, that will become a constant worry. We do not have any empire that we need someone to inherit. And if you think that you need to have children to look after us in our old age, forget it. What the hell have I have been doing for my mother other than sending money? If you are worried about who will perform our shraddha, then it is a foolish thought. I did not perform my father's shraddha. Let us work hard, and start a charitable trust that can help many needy children. Besides, the doctor hasn't said that it is impossible. We shall wait and see.'

'Shri, I don't want to wait any more. Can we adopt a child?'

Shrikant suddenly became very serious. 'Shrimati, think again. Other people's children will never be ours. We naturally tend to pardon our own children's mistakes, but it will not be possible to do that with someone else's. I am not comfortable with that idea, somehow. Shrimati, you are an intelligent person. Use your energy for more constructive work.'

Shrimati was stunned by Shri's words.

The very thought that she wouldn't experience motherhood was hurting her deeply.

After a very long time, Shrikant received a letter from Ravi Patil. Shrikant was now one of the prominent persons in his field in India and abroad. He had a secretary, Ms Priya, in the office. Over a period of time, he required someone at home too, who was smart, reliable and able to take responsibility and most importantly, intelligent and obedient. Shrimati soon became the extremely efficient personal secretary that Shrikant Deshpande had wanted at home. Shrikant did not have to create an official position for her. It was the obedient, understanding and helpful nature of Shrimati that had made Shrikant hand over such grave responsibilities to her. She believed that Shrikant was doing a great job and it was her duty to help him.

In addition to looking after his personal correspondence, she had to be a good hostess to Shrikant's personal and official guests too. Shrikant would merely sign all the letters that Shrimati would prepare. Shrimati had learnt basic computer skills and was able to use the internet and e-mail too.

After much coaxing, Gangakka had been persuaded to visit them in Bombay. Thereafter, she made many trips. Her favourite part of the house was the balcony. She would not travel by bus or train any more. She would only fly.

The success and prosperity of her son had made Gangakka more arrogant. However, she did not change her mind about Shrimati. She still thought it was bad luck that her son had married Shrimati.

As she held Ravi's letter in her hands, Shrimati's mind went back to the good old Hubli days.

Once upon a time, all of them were so close to each other but now, everyone was in their own world. Mallesh was married and had two daughters. He was running his father's oil shop successfully and had amassed a lot of black money. He had gone on a world tour with his wife and on the way back had stayed with them in Bombay. They had talked about their schooldays and the boys' vs girls' team jokes.

Jokingly, Mallesh had said, 'I have two daughters so I am in the girls' team now.'

Shrimati noticed that though Mallesh had once been a very close friend of his, Shrikant hardly spoke to Mallya in a free and frank manner. It was Shrimati who spoke all the time.

Ravi had been in the US for a long time now. His father would still convert the dollar salary into rupees and tell everyone how much his son was earning. Shrimati started reading the letter.

Dear Shrikant,

I don't remember when I had written to you last. The gap has not been intentional but only due to the changes in our address.

My father informs me once in a while about your progress. But the other day when I saw you at the conference on software technology at SFO on CNN, I was delighted. You have not changed much physically. But you have achieved great things in life. Your talk on the computer industry in the Third World was great. My hearty congratulations to you. Your speech had such authority and was very effective. I remembered our conversation on the train, the day we left IIT.

Shrikant, there are very few achievers in life. Those who achieve what they set out to, are even more rare. What you have dreamt, you have realized. My heart jumps with joy. I also remember 'the other hand of yours' who is behind your success. She has been unassuming, undemanding, and totally submissive to your needs and to your achievements. Shrikant, without her, you would not have been what you are today.

Let me write something about myself. Perhaps it is not an achievement at all in the worldly way. As you know, I used to read about psychology a lot in my IIT days. After coming to this country, I started studying more psychology than engineering. In our country, the future of children is decided by the parents! The reason could be our economic and social conditions. Parents feel that if the child does not take up engineering or medicine, then he or she cannot survive. They don't care what the child really wants. After coming here, I realized that I prefer psychology to engineering and so I changed my subject. My decision made my father very angry. He thought I had gone mad. My sisters were equally upset and sent me tearful letters. However, I am in a country where such pressures are not important, so I did what I liked.

I have completed my Ph.D and am working as a psychology professor in a college. In this rich country where personal freedom is more important, there are weak social bonds. So, there are a lot more psychological issues. Though I would like to come back to India, my profession might not fetch me the right job, so I am continuing here.

I hope you receive this letter because I have picked up your address from *Computer World* magazine. Kindly reply.

When I think of Shrimati, I continue to be amazed by her clear thinking and her wise decisions, like when she chose to join arts college in spite of getting the first rank in her tenth board exams. Do you remember that we had laughed at her? Now when I look back, I feel she was the brightest. She knew what she liked and she did exactly that. Shrikant, you are very lucky to get such a companion.

What is the news of the rest of our friends? Anthony is in the merchant navy. I met him two years back. Vasudev Shenoy left engineering and joined the IAS. He is in Delhi. I heard that you visit the US often. The next time you are here, please call me on this number, 215-386-6660. I would like to meet you and Shrimati whenever I am in India. Please remember me to Shrimati.

> Yours affectionately,
> Ravi

Shrimati was disturbed after reading Ravi's letter. Of late her self-esteem had gone down so much that she wondered whether she really deserved all of Ravi's compliments. If she was so clear in her thinking, then why was she so disturbed? She didn't know.

Shrimati wanted Shrikant to read Ravi's letter and talk about it. So she kept it next to his plate on the dining table. In her heart of hearts she hoped Shri would read the compliments that Ravi had paid her and say a few words of praise to her.

Shrikant did read the letter and without any emotion, he said, 'Please enter the contact details in my personal diary and our system.'

Shrimati was disappointed.

Shrikant got busy preparing the statistical data of his company as he was to leave for a business tour round the world. After this trip the company was planning to list its shares on the stock exchanges of other countries. So, this tour was crucial.

Recently, the company had adopted the ESOP plan. The ESOP concept had been recently introduced in India. When a company went public, all employees got a stock option, as a result of which they all became shareholders of the company. The employees of Shrikant's company were very happy because it was seen as a great incentive to continue to work in that company. Shrikant being one of the oldest employees had been offered a very large chunk of the stock. Because of that Shrikant had become a millionaire. It was very rare for a lower-middle-class person to become so rich in such a short time. It was ironical that though he was not obsessed with money, it had come to him.

Shrimati was unwell. She was suffering from the flu, and it had left her extremely weak. In spite of that she had to do Shrikant's packing. He was going to be away for a month so she had to make sure he had everything he would need.

Shrikant and Shrimati had now moved up into the neo-rich circle. She had two drivers, a cook and a maid to help with the housework. Shrikant now owned a brand new Mercedes Benz. Shrimati too had her own car and driver.

Shrikant had wanted to shift to South Bombay—the prestigious Cuffe Parade or Malabar Hill—as his status had changed. But it would take a long time to find a proper house with all the documents in order and Shrikant did not have so much time. He asked Shrimati to talk to a good real estate agent and check out what was available while he was away. However, Shrimati did not show much interest.

Shrikant noticed that Shrimati was very unwell and was quite upset. 'Shrimati, you don't listen to me at all. All the time you sit in the balcony and watch the sea. The sea breeze has affected you. If you fall ill now, how can I go? My schedule will be upset and our company will suffer. Do you realize how important this is?'

'Shri, there is no connection between me watching the sea and you going abroad. Regardless of my health, you must go,' Shrimati told him patiently.

To which Shrikant replied in a gentle tone, 'Shrimati, that was not the reason. If you are unwell and if I am out of town, it worries me. However, if you need anything, please contact Harish.'

Harish was Shrikant's junior colleague in the company. But they were close to each other as they had been classmates at IIT. Such things happened in the corporate world. Your classmates could become your subordinates. Capability is measured in terms of the success in one's career! Shrimati herself was the prefect example. Once upon a time she was considered much brighter than Shrikant, but now she could not be compared with him in any respect.

After Shrikant left, Shrimati went to bed again. Silently she prayed, let Shrikant cancel his tour and come back. Let there be some problem with the aircraft so that Shrikant is unable to go, she thought. That day she wanted someone to sit next to her and comfort her, someone who would come and stay with her. She missed her mother.

The next day, her temperature increased and Shrimati found it difficult to breathe. She was supposed to visit Vandana that week, but knew she would not be able to go. She was sleeping all alone in the huge, beautifully done-up bedroom.

The cook was on leave and the maid went away in the evening after she finished her work.

Shrimati could not sleep. She kept thinking, if I die, no one would even know. What kind of a life is this. It was so empty, so lonely in spite of all the wealth that Shrikant had earned!

The next morning, her maid Champa came as usual and rang the doorbell. But nobody answered the door. Champa got scared and went to the neighbour, Mr Jamshed Mehta, as he had an extra set of keys for the house. Mrs Mehta came with the key and opened the door. She was shocked to see that Shrimati had a very high fever and was in a stupor. She called up Nanavati Hospital and Shrikant's company. Arrangements were made to admit her immediately. Harish, his wife Prabha and Vandana rushed to the hospital.

Dr Patel, one of the seniormost doctors told them, 'Nothing to worry. She needs proper medication and rest. Can anyone stay with the patient?'

Vandana got worried and told Harish, 'Please call up Shrikant. If something goes wrong, then . . .'

But Harish knew Shrikant's nature very well. He wouldn't come unless there was an emergency. So he told the doctor, 'Mr Deshpande is out of the country and it will be some time before he can come back. Please arrange for a private nurse, and never mind the expenses.'

Vandana was shocked. In her middle-class circle she could not imagine any husband leaving his wife when she was so sick. She remembered her own case. When she had gone into labour and the pain was unbearable, her husband Pramod had stood by her side comforting her and encouraging her. After the delivery he had taken a month off to stay with her. The doctors in the hospital teased her saying that Pramod had suffered more than Vandana!

Vandana looked at her dear friend lying there, almost unconscious. For the first time, she pitied Shrimati.

A handsome young husband who was extremely ambitious, travelling throughout the year, and in-laws who only spoke ill of her. Not even a child for company! Vandana's mother often envied Shrimati's life but Vandana had never felt that way. Today more than ever she appreciated her luck and was grateful that her life was a million times better than Shrimati's. There was so much love, affection and kindness in her life unlike Shrimati's. She wondered how Shrimati had lived with such odds!

After a couple of days, Shrimati recovered her strength and was overjoyed to see her friend Vandana next to her. Vandana insisted that Shrimati should come to her house and rest for a few days, but Shrimati refused, knowing it would mean extra work for her friend. Also, Vandana's children were small.

After a week in hospital, Shrimati returned home. The first thing she had told Harish when she felt a little better in the hospital was not to inform Shrikant about her illness. She knew it would affect his state of mind and he would not be able to concentrate on his work.

Harish was surprised. If his wife Prabha were in the same situation, she would have called up at least ten times, scared him and created a scene. And he too would not have stayed away from her on office work in such a case.

But he realized that Shrimati was an exceptional woman. She cared so much for her husband and respected his work that she never created any problem that would affect his career. He thought she was like the lady who carries a torch and removes all the obstacles on the road to success for her husband.

Shrikant had taken her for granted. He had a rare diamond in his hand but he was searching for a worthless glass of achievement.

Sudha Murty

Dear Shrimati,
  Sorry for not having replied to your earlier letter. As usual I was in some part of the globe doing some work. I received your New Year card, and though late, Dorothy and I thank you very much. Our warm regards to you and Shrikant.

Shrimati, a long time ago you had talked about the historical and architectural monuments of your country. You may not remember it but I do. You had told me that one requires at least six months to take a tour of your country. Right now, I have three months' time and I have decided to visit India. My heart yearns to see the places that you had described.

It would be a great pleasure if you could accompany me on my travels, but if you have any work, then can you please arrange my itinerary and accommodation? I am coming to Bombay directly.

I will wait for your reply.

Yours affectionately,
Mike Collins

Shrimati was delighted to receive this letter. Probably he was the only foreign guest whose company she enjoyed. Most of the guests she had to entertain were Shrikant's business associates who looked at India from a very different angle.

For them, India meant cheap software. Their itinerary was to sunbathe in Goa, see the Taj Mahal, buy tonnes of silver jewellery, stay at The Oberoi—that's all. They didn't really understand what India meant nor were they interested in knowing.

Shrimati disliked people like that, but it didn't bother Shrikant very much. When they were invited for dinner, the handsome Shrikant would smile charmingly and say, 'Oh it was a great pleasure meeting you today' or 'You have made my day'. Shrimati would feel like walking out of the dinner party but she was aware that as Mrs Shrikant Deshpande, the wife of the company's director, her presence was important.

Since Shrikant was going to be out of the country, Shrimati was happy that she could join Professor Collins on his trip. Suddenly she felt she had grown wings. Her spirits soared and she felt like singing with the koel in springtime. Enthusiastically she made all the travel plans and waited for Professor Collins's arrival.

She went to the airport to receive Professor Collins personally. She was meeting him after five years. He looked a little older but was as energetic as ever. The pursuit of knowledge had kept him young.

Shrimati had planned for their journey to start at Delhi and end in Bombay. Their first destination was Fatehpur Sikri, Akbar's capital city. When they visited the fort there, Shrimati described to Professor Collins several significant historical events that had taken place at that fort.

'Sir, don't you feel that there is a difference between the Agra Fort and this small fort? It seems the Mughals shifted their capital from here to Agra due to shortage of water. When Akbar the Great did not have a male child, he prayed to the Sufi saint Salim Chishti for a son. He did

Sudha Murty

get a son and out of gratitude, named him Salim. Even today, people come and pray at the tomb for their wishes to be fulfilled. They make a knot with a piece of thread and tie it on the window grille and when the wish is fulfilled, they come back and untie the knot. This saint's tomb is here, in the fort.'

From Agra they went to Ujjain in Madhya Pradesh. She explained the importance of this city to the professor.

'Sir, Ujjain is a place with a very rich history. If one knows and loves Sanskrit, one cannot miss reading about Ujjain. It appears in all of Kalidasa's plays. Kalidasa was a great Sanskrit scholar who belonged to Ujjain. Once upon a time this place was called Avantika. Goddess Avanti was the presiding deity of this area. This is also a place where the romance between Princess Vasavadatta and Udayana bloomed. In his younger days, Emperor Ashoka was the governor of this land. It seems his beautiful wife Vidisha was from the neighbouring town. His famous children Sanghamitra and Mahendra were born here. This place is extremely important for Hindus. The Mahakaleshwar Jyotirlinga's shrine in Ujjain is one of the famous jyotirlingas of India. The myths say that there was a mysterious aura of light around the linga . . .'

Professor Collins interrupted her, 'Shrimati, is Ujjain not a strange name?'

'Yes, Sir. Some historians believe Utkarsha Jaya, that is, "the great victory" was the root name for Ujjain. Others believe it was Udatta Jain.'

From there they went to Mandu. There Shrimati related to Professor Collins the famous legend of Raja Baj Bahadur and Rani Roopmati. Their story is one of the greatest romances of Indian literature. Mandu also has beautiful palaces named after Hindustani ragas, she told him.

As they went along Shrimati explained everything from two perspectives, one from the local folk tales and the other from important historical events.

By the time they finished the north India tour, almost two months had passed. Meanwhile, Shrikant had returned to India and wanted Shrimati to come back home. He had some important guests and Shrimati was required to receive them, and be the hostess since they were important clients.

Shrimati was disappointed. She arranged for a proper guide and made sure all the arrangements for the remaining one month were in place so that Professor Collins would have no difficulties before he returned to Bombay.

When he came back to Bombay after an exhausting and exhaustive tour, Professor Collins was a little tired physically, but mentally felt fully charged. He declared that though he was seventy years old he was still young at heart.

Professor Collins had made extensive notes during his travels. He had some ideas about what he would do with them.

Shrimati had gone through all his notes and some of them she had appreciated and some others she had criticized. She was very happy about his visit but now she was sad that he was leaving. She would go back to being lonely once again.

Professor Collins was to leave for Karachi the next day but since Shrikant was in Bangkok, they were unable to meet.

After supper, Professor Collins and Shrimati sat in the balcony, watching the sea. Today, the sea did not soothe Shrimati. Professor Collins broke the silence.

'Shrimati, what are you thinking of?'

'My loneliness. Sometimes it is very depressing.'

'Shrimati, may I give you some advice? Hope you will not mind. One should have the basic happiness within oneself. That happiness comes from confidence, and confidence comes from the kind of work one does whole-heartedly.

'I have noticed that you have not lost your love for history. I have been observing you ever since I have known you. I remember how you described Badami and Sravanabelagola and Ajanta and Ellora many years ago. How you approached the monuments and places of historical significance on this trip was also commendable. You have become more mature. You are no longer as emotional about history, you have developed a critical and analytical approach.

'I had thought that marriage, this kind of wealth, family responsibilities would have made you dull, lazy and arrogant. But you are still very sensible, your attitude to life has not changed. If anything, your thoughts seem to go deeper and have become clearer.

'Shrimati, if you want to do a Ph.D even now, you can do it. Age is not a bar. I will get you a scholarship. A person like you can always pick up the threads.

'But the decision has to be yours, your personal choice. I only wanted to tell you to think it over.'

Professor Collins paused and looked at her face. There was sadness and there was immeasurable helplessness.

He continued, 'In life, everyone is not blessed with intelligence. People who have intelligence do not use it properly. I am surprised to see that you are leading such a fruitless life. If you hold water in your hand it trickles away. Your intelligence too is trickling away with time. If Dorothy were here, I would have said the same thing to her. Maybe my culture is different so I view everything in that way. Living like this may be very common in your culture.'

Shrimati did not reply and Professor Collins did not continue.

Shrimati went to the airport to see off Professor Collins. When the security check announcement was made, she looked at him. He was old and tired but his life was pure and clean, like a hermit's life. The thirst for knowledge was the breath of his life and there was no guile, deceit or manipulation or any other desire in him. That is why he could look at everyone with a compassionate heart.

Though he wasn't related to her, nor belonged to her country, the kind of concern Professor Collins showed her reminded Shrimati of her mother Kamala. Unknowingly, tears filled her eyes. She opened the bag that she was carrying and presented Professor Collins with a beautifully embroidered Kashmiri shawl.

'Sir, when you are working on your research, or whenever you feel cold, you can use this. Let it remind you of me though I stay thousands of miles away.'

'Shrimati, I don't require a shawl to remember you by. Whenever I see any student who is bright and sharp, I think of you.'

There was a final call for passengers to go to security. Suddenly Shrimati bent down and touched his feet. It was a spontaneous gesture, showing all the respect and regard she felt for him.

Professor Collins was taken aback. He patted her shoulders and said, 'May god bless you, my child,' and walked away.

twenty-one

Jacob and Dolly Lynes were coming to India. Jacob was the president of an American company with a business interest in Shrikant's company. Most of the revenue that the company earned came from America. So Shrikant was very careful in the way he treated his American clients. He was aware that a software project that was designed in India would fetch much more profit than it would if it was done in America. Shrikant's company had to set a good track record if it wanted to be listed on the New York Stock Exchange.

Shrikant had decided to host a dinner in honour of Jacob and Dolly Lynes in one of the restaurants at the Oberoi Towers at Nariman Point. To such parties, Shrikant would invite leading businessmen, industrialists, government officials—all the who's who. The purpose of these dinners was not to eat, but to develop contacts.

Normally, the invites were printed in the names of Shrimati and Shrikant. Shrimati had to play the dutiful hostess, welcome everyone with a smile and see that all the guests were comfortable. She had to talk to everybody and make them feel important.

A week had passed since Professor Collins had left India. Shrimati started thinking more and more about history. She realized that she missed studying the subject. At home, searching for some important papers she came across Ravi's letter once again. That disturbed her even more. Ravi had written that Shrimati was clear in her thinking. Was she really clear? If that was so, why was she getting so upset of late? She felt a vacuum within herself, that the work she was doing was against her wishes, that she wasn't enjoying it. She asked herself the reason for feeling this way. Then she suddenly realized that she had never enjoyed attending parties. But she could not stay away from them either. Like that evening's dinner. The thought made her even more unhappy. It was a difficult situation. If she refused to attend, Shrikant would get upset, and if she went she would be upset.

That day, for the first time, she decided not to go for the dinner. She called up Shrikant's office. Priya answered the phone.

Priya, Shrikant's secretary, was extremely efficient. She loved her job and worked as hard as two people. 'Priya, will you put Shrikant on the line please, I want to speak to him.'

Shrimati was aware that personal messages should not be passed through the secretary as it could lead to gossip.

'Sorry, madam, sir is on a video conference.'

'All right, Priya, but inform him that I had called.'

Shrimati was angry. Was his wife's call not important enough for him? He could have excused himself and come out for a minute. There were others there who were also part of the conference. For a minute she was upset with Priya, but she soon realized that she had just been doing her duty.

Shrimati was so used to doing whatever she was told that being obedient had become a habit. It often upset her greatly, yet she could not disobey instructions.

Shrimati was exhausted—mentally and physically. She felt she had to get out of the house.

She took her car out and was about to drive off when her driver, smoking a beedi with the other drivers in the basement, came running towards her. She waved him off, saying she wanted to drive herself.

She did not know where she was going. Without thinking she found herself on the road to Juhu beach. Once there, she parked the car and decided to take a walk along the shore.

It was afternoon and there were hardly any people on the beach. Had it been evening there wouldn't have been any place to stand! She saw a few teenage couples who had obviously bunked college. Probably it was the best time of their lives. Shrimati too remembered her college days and she became even more upset. Shrikant would make up excuses to tell his mother and come to meet her at the botanical gardens. They would walk up to the Taiwac watch company compound. Shrimati would have her classes only three-times a week, but when Shrikant was in town, she would come to college all the six days. When Shrikant was in town he would not miss going to the University even on a single day. They would talk endlessly. Though they did not have money at that time, they had so much to talk about. Shrikant did all the talking and she listened to him. Shrikant would tell her about his college, his friends and professors, his studies, the extracurricular activities and all about his life at IIT. Though Shrimati hadn't met any of the people he talked about, she felt she knew them because she had heard so much about each person.

Those had indeed been beautiful days.

What had happened to Shrikant now? The love, affection and sharing of ideas and dreams had disappeared. He hardly talked to her about the company or other business matters. The only time he spoke to her was to assign a list of chores for her to do. For him she had undergone so much opposition, criticism and nastiness from her in-laws. She had even given up her career, only because she really loved him. But Shrikant was not the same person she knew before their marriage. This Shrikant Deshpande was only interested in name, fame, position and status. In building up his business, he had forgotten his dear wife. This Shrikant appeared a stranger to her. Where could she find her old 'Shri'?

Shrimati sat on a wooden bench and gave vent to her grief. She sobbed uncontrollably, unmindful of the people around her. But this was Bombay. Nobody would come and ask her what the matter was, or try to console her. Shrimati realized that her memories were making her unhappy, instead of soothing her. She felt she could not sit on the beach any longer. She wanted to go somewhere else. She wiped her tears and went to the car. It was like a heated oven. She felt like going to meet Vandana. But she did not want to go unannounced. She realized that Pramod might have taken casual leave from work to be with his family. She did not want to disturb them. Shrikant never used his casual leave. He worked all the days of the week. Even his earned leave was hardly ever taken.

Heaving a deep sigh, Shrimati decided to go back home.

When she walked in, her maid Champa told her, 'Madam, there was a phone call from saab.' She was in no mood to talk to Shrikant. But her duty-conscious mind did not allow her to ignore the message. Maybe he had some important work for her. Otherwise he would not call her from the office.

When she called, Shrikant was not there but he had left a message with Priya. 'Sir wants you to bring his wallet, which he has forgotten at home.' Hearing that made Shrimati more upset. When she did not say anything, Priya asked, 'Madam, are you there? Is everything all right?' Quickly, Shrimati replied, 'Yes, Priya, thank you,' and disconnected the phone.

By the time Shrimati reached Oberoi Towers, some of the guests had already arrived. Shrikant looked very annoyed because Shrimati was late. It was her duty to come early and receive the guests. Shrimati noticed his expression but ignored it. She looked pale and tired. And unenthusiastic. That made Shrikant even more angry, though he did not show it. He introduced her to some new guests. Instead of shaking hands as usual, that day Shrimati folded her hands, said 'Namaskar,' and smiled. Shrikant added, 'We are pleased to meet you.' Shrimati was very tempted to say, 'I am extremely unhappy at meeting people like you and wasting my time.' But she could not say that. She was, after all, the wife of the director of the company. She smiled artificially and said, 'I am glad to meet you.'

Waiters with drinks were doing the rounds amidst the groups of conversing men and women. Dining was a mere formality. After her first such party, Shrimati was taken aback at seeing the bill.

'Isn't it too much, Shri?' she asked. 'The food wasn't very good either.'

Laughing at her ignorance, Shrikant had replied, 'Don't apply your Hubli norms to such a party. The amount of money we spend at these parties is a pittance compared to the business we get.'

Every dinner, every conversation, every relationship was based on profit and loss. What a way to live, she had thought!

Shrimati was reminded of that conversation once again. She was lost in deep thought when Harish's wife Prabha came and tapped her shoulder. 'Shrimati, where are you lost?' Prabha, an MA in sociology, was from Agra. She had a six-year-old son, Amol, who was in a boarding school in Kodaikanal in Tamil Nadu.

'Oh hello, Prabha, I didn't see you,' Shrimati said. 'How is Amol? Do you miss him?' she asked.

She had managed to evade Prabha's question. The talkative Prabha replied, 'To be very frank with you, Shrimati, I am happy that he is in boarding school. It is a very disciplined life, and he has lots of company. As an only child he gets bored and was beginning to get a little stubborn. Besides, we only talk in Hindi at home. There he will learn to speak excellent English.'

Prabha was a friendly, open, person. Though Shrimati and she were different in nature they were very good friends. Prabha did not take life seriously. She did not think too deeply about anything either. Whenever Harish went on tour, she would go to Agra. She had a big friends' circle even in Bombay. All of them would often go out for lunch or shopping.

'Prabha, why don't you have another child? Amol will also have company.'

'Are you mad, Shrimati! I had a lot of problems during pregnancy and I do not want to go through it again. '

The conversation was interrupted by Meher Engineer.

'Hi, Shrimati! You are looking so beautiful. How do you manage to stay so slim? Do you go to Figurette at Bandra? It seems all film stars go there. I wish I were in Bandra,' Mrs Engineer said wistfully, looking down at her obese body. Mr Engineer was a well-known builder.

They were joined by Prema Malhotra, wife of an advertising executive. 'Shrimati! How nice to see you again.

What are your plans for the weekend? It seems there is a diamond jewellery exhibition on at Tribhuvandas Zaveri. All of us have decided to go. Why don't you come with us?' she said.

'Sorry, I may not be able to come. Shri might be at home.'

'Oh c'mon Shrimati! You behave like a perfect housewife. When our men don't bother about us and travel all the time for their work, we also should spend our time the way we want.' That was the advice given by the elderly, in fact seniormost lady, Indumathi Sukhtankar.

Shrimati was feeling sick. Sarees, jewellery always brought her bad memories. They would remind her of Gangakka's taunts. Gangakka wanted her daughter-in-law to be simple but her daughter could wear the best of sarees and loads of gold ornaments. If Shrimati bought an expensive saree, Gangakka would shout at her for wasting Shrikant's money.

Rama had an indirect way of mocking her, 'Shrimati, for your complexion, pearl jewellery might be better than gold!' suggesting that Shrimati was darker than Shrikant. But there is no use thinking of all that now, thought Shrimati, and went back to the guests.

Shrikant had noticed that his wife was not her normal self that day and on the pretext of taking his wallet from her, he went up to Shrimati and softly but firmly told her in Kannada, 'Shrimati, what's wrong with you? You have not spoken to Jacob! Go and talk to him and his wife immediately.'

The chief guests for the evening, Jacob and Dolly Lynes, had arrived a few minutes earlier. Dolly had an artificial smile on her lips. She was a party person. She attended and hosted a hundred such parties throughout the year.

Shrimati went up to them and with a smile, greeted them. After some small talk, Dolly said to Shrimati, 'It seems you are very knowledgeable in history? You must have got your doctorate in America. '

Shrimati replied curtly, 'No, I am just an MA from my hometown.'

'Oh, is that so? Then how did you manage to acquire so much knowledge and sophistication?'

Shrimati did not bother to answer that question.

For Dolly, the answer was not important. She was just making conversation.

'Well, Shrimati, then you must study the ancient and splendid history of America.'

'Excuse me, Dolly. Your history is neither ancient nor splendid. The success of America is the result of technical progress and implementation of the innovative ideas that were born in some other country. Your country's history is the youngest in the world.'

'I don't understand . . .'

'Take the example of SAP software. It was innovated in Germany but implemented in the US and today the whole world thinks it is an American invention . . .'

Shrikant's sharp ears caught Shrimati's cold and harsh remarks.

What was Shrimati talking about? This was not the kind of thing to say at a party. Dolly was the power behind Jacob. Why argue with such a person?

Here he was trying to please everyone, and there was Shrimati being so blunt. Shrikant was worried that she might spoil things for him and ruin his business dealings. A man of great common sense, he knew that if someone's clothes were stuck on a thorn bush, it was better to gently free the garment than pull it off.

Shrikant joined the conversation.

'Hello, Dolly! You look wonderful! How was your trip to Jaipur?'

This was an indication for Shrimati to stop being blunt. But she deliberately ignored it.

'Oh, Shrikant, it was lovely. I can see so much Western influence in India. Look at the name of this room for instance. It is such a beautiful French name.'

Neither Dolly nor Shrikant knew what *La Giaconda* meant.

Shrimati could not resist. 'It is not a mere French name. It is the name of the world-famous painting of Leonardo da Vinci, the *Mona Lisa*, the lady with the enigmatic smile. It is her the room is named after. If one goes to Paris and one has the time and the inclination to visit the Louvre, one can see the *Mona Lisa* there.'

Shrikant was taken aback. He felt that this was an insult to Dolly. Shrimati was not behaving like a charming hostess. On the contrary, she was being rude to his guest!

How did it matter if it was *La Giaconda* or *Mona Lisa*. Getting business was Shrikant's ultimate intention.

The party went on as usual. Shrikant did not disturb Shrimati again.

While returning from the party, Shrikant was not his placid self. He was fuming. He wanted to talk to Shrimati. He could not wait till they reached home so he started the conversation in Kannada. Even in that situation he took care that Maruthi, his driver, should not understand the contents of the conversation.

'Shrimati, what is the matter with you? Why did you insult Dolly? Who wanted your knowledge of history?'

'Shri, I did not go there to exhibit my knowledge. For that matter, I did not even want to go. Even if I had wanted to show off, there was no one there who would have understood it. Look at Dolly! Look at her arrogance! The way she looks down upon India—she believes that we have to learn everything from their country. Look at Professor Collins or Dorothy. They are so knowledgeable and yet humble. Education should bring simplicity and modesty.'

'Enough of your lecture, Shrimati. Don't talk about your worthless subject. The world of business is so different from yours. History cannot feed you. Don't behave like a historian at such parties. You should remember that you represent our company and must be loyal to it. After all, what is there in India's history to boast so much about?' Shrikant paused.

Shrimati was tremendously hurt. She did not answer. Whatever language they had spoken in, Maruthi would know that husband and wife were quarrelling. When they reached home, Shrikant changed into his night-dress and picked up the *Economic Times*. He usually glanced at the headlines in the morning as there wasn't enough time to read in detail. But at night he read it carefully. That day, he was so upset by the incident that though he was holding the paper, he was unable to read.

Shrimati was more upset than him. Her mind was seething. For the first time in ten years of marriage, Shrikant had attacked her individual freedom. What had he said? Shrimati recalled his words. *Don't talk about your worthless history. The world of business is so different from yours. History cannot feed you. Don't behave like a historian at such parties. You should remember that you represent our company . . . After all, what is there in India's history to boast so much about?*

She too could have said many things to him, 'Shri, do not forget that you are not only the director of a company. You are also the husband of Shrimati who is sensitive and sentimental about Indian history. Do not measure everything in terms of profit and loss.' But she had not said that. She had never talked ill of anybody, or deliberately hurt Shrikant. But today his sharp words had chopped the tender tree of their relationship.

Shrimati snatched the paper that Shrikant was trying to read.

'Shri, tell me what was your intention in saying all that in the car? I have not done anything to bring down your prestige.' The normally quiet Shrimati was bursting like a cracker torched by a flame. She was so upset and emotional that her hands were trembling. Shrikant took her hands and made her sit next to him. He was cool and calculative in his words. 'Shrimati, we Indians live on our past glory. Once upon a time, it is said, India was the most prosperous country, the land of honey and nectar. Diamonds and pearls were sold on the streets of Hampi. The doormen of Nalanda University would conduct the entrance examinations for students. Whether there is any truth in that or not, I do not know. But these are things of the past. Forget the past. What we are today is what is relevant and important.We have a very rigid caste system, superstitions abound and to top it all, a highly corrupt society. Look at the West. They are scientific, systematic and progressive. You talk so much about history, let me ask you a simple question. Which is more important, the Kalinga war which your Emperor Ashoka fought or present-day terrorism which we have to stop? We must think of the ways by which we can make India a modern, scientific and developed country.

'Shrimati, you talk so much about Ashoka and idolize him. What has he done? He embraced Buddhism. Hence, his army became weak. Subsequently, he never fought a war to protect his country. Eventually, his empire was destroyed by his enemies. Because of his attitude we lost our country to invaders.'

Shrikant was criticizing Shrimati's favourite subject and belittling her hero, Ashoka. Though Shrikant did not know much about Ashoka, he said all that because he wanted to hurt Shrimati. Business had taught him that. To insult a person, you don't need to attack him or her directly, one can do that instead by attacking what that person admires or respects. Though Shrikant had spoken calmly and coolly, he was still fuming inside. He went to the refrigerator and drank a glass of water to hide his anger.

Shrimati's fury knew no bounds. 'Shri, what are you trying to suggest? Do you mean history is a subject of the dead, the lost and the defeated? Does the past not have any relevance to the present, according to you? You are

Sudha Murty

wrong. It does. A company's past can say what a company's future can be, only in your language it is called "track record"! You gave me the example of Ashoka, but what do you know about him? One shouldn't talk about anything without knowing enough about the subject. For a person like you who always calculates everything, understanding such a great human being is way beyond your ability. Ashoka never tried to immortalize himself. His deeds made him great. When an empire falls, there are various reasons for it. The successors of the emperor might not be good. The invader might be mighty. Just a strong army cannot win a war. What happened to Allauddin Khilji who extended his kingdom from Delhi to Rameswaram by sheer power of the sword? His empire vanished within four years of his death. A benevolent king like Shivaji made a great impact with his small army against the mighty Mughals. For a failure, there are many complex reasons. And for your information, war is not the only solution.

'Shri, you have visited Boston. You have visited Delhi. Boston is not older than Delhi. But the historical sense of Americans makes them preserve all the historical monuments of Boston. Have you not seen the Freedom Trial in Boston? How many of us would like to keep our monuments like them? Every small country in Europe is extremely proud of its history and will make every effort to preserve and showcase it.'

Shrimati paused and swallowed deeply. Her face was flushed with emotion. She then continued, 'Over a period of time, the superstitions of a culture grow on to become a habit. The older the civilization, the greater the superstitious beliefs and hence slower the progress. It is like a wave. Older civilizations, like Egypt, China and India, are rigid unlike America. Just as there are ups and downs in the life of an individual, the same is true for a country.'

Shrimati paused and looked at Shrikant. She had never spoken so much with such feeling. Shrikant was surprised. He looked at her as if he was seeing her for the first time. Shrimati had not finished. She remembered the way he had whipped her with his words and she continued.

'Don't think Western countries do not have superstitions and that they are always rational. Why is number thirteen considered a bad number? Why do they say walking under a ladder brings bad luck? And why do young girls rush to catch the bride's bouquet? One should think logically about why we have remained economically backward. A bright person like you who is in business can understand it very well. You don't require a historian's help. When the Industrial Revolution took place, we were slaves of the British. They destroyed our home industries so that we would have to buy their products. A stepmother will never love her stepchildren. So the British never bothered about the industrialization of our country. Please do not think that industrialization is such a great thing. It loosens social bonding, brings in a disparity between the haves and have nots and most importantly, leads to psychological disorders.'

Shrimati stopped talking. Shrikant was still listening to her. This time, Shrimati drank water.

She continued, her voice softening. 'Shri, please look at your dress, and the English language that you speak most of the time. Is it not a witness to the victory of British colonization, even after many years of independence?'

This was too much for Shrikant. He was dumbstruck. He had never expected Shrimati to lash out at him with such harsh words. She would usually cry and keep quiet but never argue with him so fiercely. As an individual, he was aware that Shrimati's arguments were clear, precise and logical, but as a husband, he was unable to digest it. It was probably the first time in the ten years of their marriage that Shrimati had shown her unhappiness and disagreement with Shrikant's way of thinking. In that instant Shrikant felt that they were two strangers living under the same roof.

Shrikant received a letter from Gangakka. She wrote, once when Shrikant was ill as a child, she had prayed for his recovery to Lord Mylaralinga. Now, the Lord had appeared in her dreams and had reminded her of her dues. So she had decided to give a golden crown to the Lord. She ordered her son to take a few days' leave and make the pilgrimage with the crown. There was no mention of Shrimati in the entire letter.

The temple of Mylaralinga, another name of Shiva or Eshwara, is situated on the hills of Devaragudda, around a hundred kilometres from Hubli. Gangakka had great faith in the family deity and believed that unless Lord Mylaralinga blessed him, Shrikant would not prosper.

Shrikant knew that his mother was very superstitious and gods appearing in her dreams was a common occurrence. He was very happy that his money could be used to fulfil his mother's wishes. Money was not an issue at all. But Shrikant being an atheist, never went with her on pilgrimages. He thought that the next time he went to Bangalore, he would visit his sister and mother at Hubli. But travelling to Hubli would take up an extra day.

While having dinner that night he told Shrimati, 'On my next visit to Bangalore, mark two days off for personal work.'

Shrimati immediately realized the reason. It irritated her. Though she tried to hide it, her unhappiness showed on her face. 'So, you are going to Hubli. Is there any special reason?'

'Not really, but I wanted to see Avva.'

'But Shrikant, I want you to take a couple of days off and sit with me to talk over many things.'

'What is there to talk for two days, Shrimati?'

'When you can spend two days for your mother's sake, can't you spend two days with me? I am all alone here.'

'That is not a new thing for you. If you want, you can come to Hubli too.'

'When your mother has not called me, why should I come? Why should I stay alone here? Has your sister stayed alone any time in her life? Your mother goes to keep her company even if she is alone for a day.'

'Shrimati, don't compare yourself with Rama. You are more educated than her.'

'Shrikant, you have one set of rules for me and another for her. Every time she gets the upper hand only because she is uneducated. Is it wrong that I am educated? Why should I have to suffer like this?'

Actually the issue was not about staying alone. It was Gangakka.

'Shri, you have time and money for your mother. I don't want your money. But I want your time.' Shrimati's anger was raging and her patience was breaking. She could not take any more insults from Gangakka.

'Avva knows that you are not happy there and you won't come. So she has not invited you.'

Shrimati started sobbing. All said and done, Shrikant was Gangakka's son. Even after ten years of marriage, he had never been Shrimati's husband. It is the duty of every mother to educate her child, regardless of the odds. Shrikant, however, believed that his mother had made an extraordinary sacrifice for him. On the other hand, all that Shrimati had done was merely the duty of a wife, and there was nothing special about it.

Shrikant picked up his files and went to his study. Shrimati was hoping that he would talk to her, console her. But he didn't. Shrimati felt suffocated. She could not stay in the same house with Shrikant. She took the house keys and walked out.

It was night and she was all alone. Hearing the sound, Shrikant knew that Shrimati had opened the front door. He shouted, 'Shrimati, don't go out alone!'

She replied coolly, 'I can manage.'

Shrikant was relieved that the quarrel had ended, and immersed himself in his files. Shrimati got out of the building and started walking down the road.

This prestigious apartment block housed executives of many companies. She wondered whether every family had fights like theirs. Was there real peace in any family? Were all these ambitious men as unconcerned about their wives' feelings? Who knows!

Nobody tells the truth about their family life. Most husbands and wives put on the appearance of being perfectly matched!

Shrimati walked up to the seaside and sat on the concrete embankment. At this hour, very few people were around. Under normal circumstances, Shrimati might have realized the danger in coming out alone at night and felt scared. But that day such things were of no importance. She just wanted to be alone. Her eyes filled with tears and rolled down her cheeks, wetting her saree. She remembered all the fights at home. The cool sea breeze ruffled her long hair and touched her face. It brought back memories of the happy days of the past.

She was dreaming once more . . .

So many flowers of splendid colours were in bloom in the month of Shravan. She could smell the fragrance of the champaka, jasmine, rajanigandha and above all, the delicate bakula . . .

Her mind was full of sensation. Her heart was full of hope and longing. She would gather all the bakula flowers and make a string that would adorn her plait. Shrikant would come. He would take the string of bakula from her hair and inhale its fragrance. He wouldn't let her wear any other flower in her hair . . .

He would always say that the flowers in her hair smelt doubly sweet . . .

The waves were crashing against the rock without rest, and so were her dreams.

She sat there for a long time, and then without warning it began to rain. It was an unseasonable shower. Shrimati was drenched. There was so much water in the sea and there was so much water in the clouds but she felt thirsty. All she needed was a few kind words from Gangakka or a few words of appreciation from her husband, to quench her thirst.

The night policeman who was patrolling the area, called out to her, 'Madam, please go home now. It is dangerous to sit here all alone.'

Shrimati was in no mood to argue. So she got up and started walking back.

When she returned home, Shrikant was still busy with his files.

By this time she had calmed down and wanted to talk to him.

'Shri, can you do me a favour?'

Shrikant was happy that his wife was her normal self again so that he could work more efficiently, with peace of mind.

'What is it, Shrimati? Is it something impossible?'

'If you make up your mind it is not difficult.'

'What is it?'

'Shrikant, you have achieved a lot in life. We have enough money for the rest of our lives. Give up this job. Let's go back to Hubli. There you had so much time for us. We can do whatever we want.'

Shrikant laughed. He pushed the files across the table and came round to where she was. Putting his arms around her, he said, 'Shrimati, are you aware of what you just said? Think rationally, and be practical. You want me to retire at the age of thirty-three! A man is in his prime at this age. It is the time for him to grow professionally. Besides, I still feel that I have not achieved much in life. I cannot live in Hubli. What would I do there? Hubli is my past. I will be like a fish out of water in Hubli, though I was born and brought up there. My present and future is in Bombay. I do not waste even a moment here.'

Shrimati did not know what to say to that.

'Shrimati, the past is always beautiful because we cannot get it back. Childhood looks beautiful when you are young. Youth looks romantic when you are old. Whatever we lose is always precious. Think of adjusting and looking forward to an ever-changing world. Don't get into the past.'

Shrimati was speechless at Shrikant's words.

Shrikant looked at her and said, 'Why are you not saying anything?'

She replied sadly, 'Shri, if you can't understand my silence, then you will not understand my words!'

Shrimati could not sleep that whole night. But Shrikant slept soundly. Things like this did not affect him. He would fall asleep as soon as he hit the bed since he worked hard all day.

Unable to sleep, Shrimati got out of bed and went to the Godrej almirah in the room. She took out the bundle of letters that Shrikant had written to her during his IIT days. She had wrapped them neatly in a silk cloth and had kept them in a sandalwood box, as if they were a great treasure. She thought if she read them she would feel better. Also, it would help her find out if it was the same Shrikant who was now her husband. She opened one of the letters and started to read it. It was the one written to her when he had seen the Taj Mahal, during the first industrial tour from the college.

My dear Shrimati,
I saw the Taj Mahal today. The city of Agra is very dirty. I do not know what you feel when you see it from your historian's viewpoint. But the immediate thought that came to my mind was how many marble slabs the builder must have used! He must have emptied many marble quarries in India. No one can build another Taj Mahal, because obviously, there won't be enough marble! I wonder how many men worked relentlessy for this project and did the emperor really pay them all! I am sure that you and I will visit this monument sometime in our life and when we do, I know you will be amazed to see it. The Taj Mahal is surrounded by a huge garden. When we come here, I want to lie down under a shady tree, my head resting on your lap, reading a computer book . . .

Shrimati smiled, forgetting where she was right now. She felt that each word in that letter was filled with affection. Affection does not require beauty or intelligence. It only requires mutual love and intense faith. That is what ultimately builds trust in any relationship.

Shrimati put the letters away, switched off the light and tried to sleep. Shrikant was snoring. Shrimati wanted to ask, *Shri where have you gone? Where have I lost you?* She felt she was searching for a path of love in the darkness, without a torch.

———————

Shrikant woke up at five in the morning. His disciplined mind could wake him up at any time. He never required an alarm. But that day, even though he was awake, he did not get out of bed. Was it more than just laziness? Was it because of what had happened the previous night? After tossing and turning for fifteen minutes, Shrikant felt that he could not afford to waste any more time. He got up and went to the kitchen to make himself a cup of tea. He did not feel like disturbing Shrimati. While having his tea in the balcony, he looked at the sea. A fresh cool morning breeze was blowing. Though it was pleasant, he felt the chill. He pulled his gown tight around him and went inside and brought Shrimati's shawl to wrap around himself. Once again he felt like watching the sea, standing in the balcony. Normally, he would never waste time like this early in the morning. He would rather make overseas calls at that hour. But that day, he did not feel like doing so. Probably this was one of the few occasions where he listened to his heart rather than his mind.

In the dawn, Bandra looked different. The fisherwomen carrying their baskets of fish, walked briskly towards the market. They were slim, well dressed and hardworking. They were the Koli community who had once upon a time, occupied all of Bombay. However, it was not just a city any more but a mega city and the economic capital of India.

Shrikant contemplated how in fifteen years Bombay had changed and so had his life. In spite of all the problems,

Bombay was most dear to him. He appreciated its cosmopolitan nature, its professional approach and work ethic. He thought if he hadn't left Hubli, he would not have been in this position!

While watching the sea, Shrikant remembered his childhood. Hubli was an inland town so the sea was unheard of. He remembered the first time that he had seen the sea, when he was about twelve years old. He had gone to Gokarna with his mother on one of her pilgrimages. It was the first time he had gone anywhere outside Hubli. He had very few relatives to visit. The only place he could go to in the holidays was his uncle Sheenappa's house.

Along with memories of his childhood, came the thought of his mother's hardships during that time. Below him, the roaring waves were dashing against the black rocks and then receding. When one wave flowed back, it merged into another one. This went on, continuously. So did Shrikant's thoughts. Once again he remembered his mother. Her only desire was that Shrikant should become an engineer and join the PWD. It was because Gangakka's role model was Shyam. Shyam used to look down upon them. Things had turned around, Gangakka was the superior one now, thanks to her son's achievements.

The sun had already risen and Bombay was bustling with activity, destroying the morning peace. But Shrikant's mind was still in turmoil. Bombay! he thought. With money, one could buy anything and everything here, except a mother's love. Shrikant knew that his mother was not educated and so she would make some rude comments. Shrimati wouldn't understand that. He felt that both Gangakka and Shrimati were not rational. He, on the other hand, was always practical. Actually Bombay made everyone practical.

People from North Karnataka are very emotional, Shrikant thought. Where people are sentimental, emotion has the upper hand. When people are emotional, practicality slackens. When a person is not practical, he or she is not able to do any business. When there is no business, there is no economic growth.

His mind went back to the family feud between his family and Shrimati's. No one really remembered the reason for it, but it still continued. Shrimati's mother Kamala was different, though.

The bakula flower came to his mind. He thought how he had not seen any for a long time. Would he be able to buy some here? He wanted to tell Shrimati to get a few for him. An efficient, resourceful person like her would definitely find them. Once she took responsibility for a job, she made sure it was completed.

As usual Shrikant left for office at eight in the morning. Due to the heavy traffic, if he delayed leaving home by even five minutes, he would get late by half an hour in reaching his office. For Shrikant, who weighed every minute, time was precious. His driver Maruthi liked to talk but Shrikant did not encourage him. He believed that a distance should be maintained between him and the driver. However, Shrimati did not believe in barriers like this and would chat with drivers and maids.

Normally, Shrikant would look at files or make calls from his mobile phone as he drove to office.

But that day he failed to do any of these things. He tried to figure out Shrimati's behaviour of late. She was no longer her calm and docile self. She would argue over silly things. She had everything in life, all the comforts and conveniences. Her mother-in-law was not staying with her, she could do what she liked, buy whatever she wanted.

To this day, Shrikant's cheque book was with her. He would ask her for money whenever he needed some. He had no bad habits—he did not drink nor did he womanize. And yet Shrimati was unhappy. She didn't want to go to any business dinners any more. The last time she had gone to Germany three months ago, she had spent three days there and enjoyed seeing the Berlin Museum. She had skipped every single business dinner. Shrikant couldn't understand what there was in the museum that so fascinated her. She had seen the best museums in the world and yet she insisted on going there every day. Shrikant had gone to Paris for three months but not once had he thought of visiting the Louvre. Suddenly the car jolted. The driver had applied the air brake. There was a huge traffic jam on the busy Peddar Road. Shrimati had so occupied Shrikant's mind that he had not noticed it. Her behaviour was bothering him. Was it her extremely sensitive attitude that was making her unhappy?

Recent incidents kept surfacing in his mind. Like when Rama had come to Bombay along with her children. Shrikant had taken all of them for dinner to the Taj. Looking at the bill, Rama had commented, 'Shrikant, the cost of your one night's dinner is equal to a month of ours.'

Shrikant had laughed but Shrimati had interpreted it as Rama indirectly hinting at their lavish spending on luxuries, while they were suffering in a small town!

Shrikant had told her, 'Shrimati, Rama has never seen a five-star hotel. So don't take her comments seriously.'

When he was young he remembered his mother spending enormous time and labour cooking with firewood and using the grinding stone. Shrimati had never had to do that—she had a cook.

And the amount Shrimati had travelled! Probably only a bird would have travelled as much!

It was possible only because Shrikant earned that kind of money. To do so, he had to work the way he had been working all these years. Even now, unless the company did well, they could not afford to pay such salaries. If the company had to be well-off, then business had to be better, and to do good business, entertaining was a must. But Shrimati refused to attend such parties. Was it not wrong?

While Shrikant pondered these thoughts, the car reached Nariman Point. Shrikant saw his office and Gangakka, Rama and Shrimati, all vanished from his mind. Computers, competition and products occupied that space.

twenty-six

A s soon as Harish saw Shrikant, he felt relieved. He hurriedly came and said, 'Shrikant, I am extremely sorry but I forgot to inform you that the state IT minister is supposed to visit our office today.'

Shrikant was upset for a second. 'How could you forget to tell me such an important thing? It is unpardonable.'

Shrikant rushed to his chamber. His room was spacious but spartan. He had an excellent aesthetic sensibility. Anyone who walked into his office, could mistake it for an American office.

Normally, Shrikant did not meet all the visitors. Only if the person was very important did Shrikant give him an appointment. When he came to know that the minister was supposed to visit, he started chalking out the programme. Over the years Shrikant had acquired extraordinary knowledge in diverse fields. He had also developed great confidence, probably the result of his phenomenal success. Success makes a person confident. But Shrikant put it in a different way: Repeated success makes a person arrogant and occasional failure makes a person confident, he would say.

Harish could not help noticing how much Shrikant had changed over the last fifteen years. When they had joined IIT, Harish was a Bombay boy and Shrikant was a small-town boy. But today, Shrikant was smarter than anyone else. He was going from strength to strength every year. He had also become a workaholic.

Initially men work for money but soon, money becomes unimportant. It is power. There is nothing like power.

Power is like liquor. Once the intoxication of power catches hold of an ambitious person, there is no escape from it. It is a vicious circle. Like in a whirlpool, it is difficult to come out of it. More work, more involvement and more power. The individual loses the ability to see and enjoy anything outside his work. He is immersed in work throughout the day. Work is his breath. What happens when such people grow old? All the pages in their book of life will be empty, except the page of achievement. Shrikant's book will contain different computer languages, different specifications and products, but nothing about his wife, family or friends.

To achieve that kind of success, one required a supportive, intelligent but docile and unambitious wife. Intelligent women are normally ambitious. Someone like Shrimati, who never ever demanded anything from her husband, was rare. Harish thought for a moment. What would have happened if Shrikant had married a person like Prabha, who was not very supportive or Rekha, who was an executive in the company? The answer was simple. Shrikant would have deserted her or she would have deserted him.

The minister's visit was over.

Harish noticed Shrikant's expression of pure joy when the minister left. 'Hey, Shrikant, how did you manage so well?' Harish asked.

'Harish, experience is my teacher and an expensive one too. Ten years ago, I joined this company as a trainee software engineer. Today I have become a director. I did not have any godfathers or any political supporters. The company does not even know to which community I belong. I have worked hard and sincerely for the benefit of the company. Not for a day have I put my personal needs or happiness before the company's. The company's success has always been more important to me than anything. There is no shortcut to success.'

Shrikant went back to his chamber. Priya was checking his diary. Harish followed him. 'Shrikant, we wanted to arrange a seminar for all our project managers at Kodaikanal. Can you inaugurate it?'

'Why such an odd place?'

'Shrikant, everyone is not like you. They want to take a break from the routine and spend time with their families. But we cannot afford to give them leave, so this will serve both the purposes.'

'That's okay. I am not the boss of my diary. Check with Priya.'

Priya said, 'Sorry, Sir. Kodai is not connected by plane and hence it is not possible. For the next two months you are busy.'

'Then, I am sorry Harish. By the way, how is Amol?'

'Oh, he is fine. We visited him recently. He does not even want to come home for a vacation. He finds it boring here. He complains that neither of us is at home, so he prefers to be in the hostel.'

Even before Harish had finished his reply, Shrikant's mind went back to his work.

'Harish, we should have a road show in the US some time. I want it on top priority. We should do it before our competitors get into the market. Kindly get back to me at the earliest once you have made the preliminary plans.'

Shrikant immersed himself in his work once again. He seldom spoke while working.

Normally Shrikant was not distracted by anything. He could focus fully as soon as he opened a file. But that day he found it difficult to concentrate. He felt like speaking to Shrimati. Their frequent quarrels were increasing the distance between them.

It is natural for any two human beings to differ. A husband and wife are no exception. In fact, if they didn't differ, then there probably was something wrong with the marriage.

The previous night, Shrimati had questioned his basic purpose in life. She showed that she did not believe in what he considered essential in life.

Whenever he wanted to talk to Shrimati, Shrikant did not ask Priya to connect him, but he would call himself. Just as he picked up the phone to dial the home number, Priya buzzed him and said that the chairman wanted to meet him urgently. Shrikant put the phone down and walked to the chairman's chamber . . .

O n the way home, Shrikant had too many matters weighing on his mind. He was mulling over the latest figures of the company's sales and budget. They wanted to have a road show but due to the crash in the computer market, it had to be postponed. In this situation it was essential for him to go to the US, spend at least two to three weeks there talking to the managers and bankers to gauge the situation. He needed to be sure they were still interested in his company.

His was not the first Indian company to be listed. Several other companies had been listed and were also doing well.

Shrikant took every challenge as an opportunity. He felt the stronger the hurricane, the greater the challenge. Shrikant believed challenges meant opportunities for growing. It was pointless worrying, action had to be taken.

He called up Priya and told her to cancel all his appointments, however important, and informed her to book a ticket for Delhi that night and to the US after a couple of days.

When he reached home, his head was heavy. He told his driver Maruthi that he would be ready in an hour's time and asked him to stay back to drop him at the airport.

He knew that Shrimati's driver would have left by then. Without even looking for Shrimati, he went to his study and picking up some papers, called out to her, 'Shrimati, I may be off to the US for two to three weeks. Kindly pack my bag. I think our friend Vasudev Shenoy and his wife are coming from Delhi on a personal visit. They are our guests. Let them stay here, not in the company's guest house. Please look after them and organize all their trips at our expense. He is an extremely useful person to us.

'Please pack an extra pair of specs and boots for me.

'I was supposed to go to Hubli for a day next month. But now, I will not be able to do so. Inform my mother about this change of plan. By the way, she has asked for some gold item. If possible, arrange for it or send the money for it.' Shrikant gave all these instructions without once looking up from his papers.

Maruthi, who had followed him into the study with his briefcase, was surprised to hear him talk like this to memsaab. He thought Shrikant's behaviour resembled his drunkard father Tukaram's. They were in their own nasha, without being bothered about others. Under intoxication, they behave like that. Look at our saab, Maruthi thought. He doesn't drink. But he behaves like he does. Maruthi thought of his young wife Tulasi. He had promised her that he would take her for a movie that night. But by the time he dropped his boss at the airport and returned, all the theatres would be closed. Tulasi would be upset, but also happy with his overtime allowance. Maruthi went downstairs.

Shrimati did not move an inch. Shrikant looked at her and said, 'Shrimati, hurry up. Serve my dinner quickly. I cannot eat on the plane, you know. I forgot to tell you! Pack two of my suits as well.'

'Shri, where are you going?'

'Didn't you hear me? I am going to the US, I said.'

'But Shri . . .'

'Please don't waste time. I am getting late.'

'I cannot do your work. I will get bored being alone for three weeks. You had promised that you would take leave for three days next month. And those three days you would not take up any official work. Because of that I booked our tickets to Ladakh.'

'Cancel them. I don't even have time to talk about it now. I have tremendous pressure from office.'

'Please, Shri, can't you postpone your tour at least this time, for my sake?'

She knew Shrikant would not do it. It had never happened before. But still she wanted to put her demand forward, to let him know that she did not want to be the lowest priority any more. Shrikant realized that Shrimati was not going to do anything for him. He himself went to the wardrobe and started taking out his clothes.

'Shrimati, don't be irrational. Tell Priya to send you my itinerary tomorrow. Pack in some aspirin and sulphur tablets. I have to leave in the next half hour.'

Shrimati was standing as still as a rock. But inside her mind, she was exploding like a volcano. She had been so happy that Shrikant had at last agreed to spend three days with her. She was looking forward to the trip with much eagerness. Now, she felt like a tired traveller in a desert, looking for an oasis. Her heart didn't want to accept that Shrikant did not care for her. But by his behaviour today she knew she was right. Shrikant was only living for himself and his ambitions. He was using her as a personal secretary at home. At least for his official secretary there were timings, but for her it was an all-time job. Her anger was increasing by leaps and bounds, superceding reason.

'Shri, you cannot go anywhere today. You always think of yourself. You are so selfish that you think only of your position, your company and your mother. You never think of me as a human being or what hurts me and what makes me happy! You treat me like a machine.

'You give appointments to everybody but you don't have any time for me. Don't I deserve one? Don't you have any duty towards me? You spend all day occupied by your company, physically and mentally. What is left for me? You give me false assurances every time and I believe you. I am neither a bank nor a post office to send money to your mother. She is related to me through you. When you do not care about me, why should I care about her? Shri, tell me now. Who is important, your wife or your profession? Ask your heart and tell me.

'I am aware that the value of a person is known only during a critical time. The time has come now and you have to decide today, now and at this very moment.'

Shrimati was overcome with emotion. She caught hold of his shirt and snatched the suitcase. The suitcase fell open and all the things scattered to the ground. Shrikant was struggling to control his rising temper.

'Shrimati, I cannot answer such a nonsensical question. I don't want to travel at my own will but the work demands it. It is your duty to support a husband like me. Now, you are emotional and being silly. Not only are you wasting your time but you are wasting my precious time too. I have many things to do. I am already late. Please let me go.'

Helpless and disappointed, Shrimati started sobbing. She didn't want him to be happy when she was so unhappy in this marriage. She wanted the heat of her unhappiness to touch him too.

'Shri, if you consider that your time is more valuable than mine, if your work is more important than my inner happiness, I will allow you to go. You do your duties to your company because you are paid and given a status.

What about my work? And what is my role in this marriage? Just think it over, whether you have discharged any responsibilities as a husband. Has your mother performed her duties as the head of the family? You decide one way or the other. You have an obligation to your wife. If you do not fulfil it, I will not stay in this house.' Shrimati was holding his hand firmly.

This was the first time that Shrimati had talked so openly about Gangakka and in relation with Shrikant's work. There was no logic. Both were entirely different issues. He was surprised by her behaviour. His watch showed that he was getting late and he would miss his flight. He could not afford to spend one day quarrelling with his wife. He forcefully freed himself and said, 'Shrimati, think whatever you want. I have told you my opinion. I am not going for my own pleasure or for extra money. Neither am I cheating on you. Shrimati, the whole world says that you are more intelligent than me. You think over it and whatever you feel is right, go ahead and do it. I am leaving now.'

Listening to Shrikant, Shrimati felt as if she had touched a live wire and stood dumbstruck. Shrikant did not eat his dinner. He took his bag and left.

Now Shrimati did not care what others would say. She ran to the balcony and shouted, 'I won't be in town for a month. I won't look after your guests.'

Though Shrikant heard it he didn't respond and just told Maruthi to drive to the domestic airport. He knew very well that she would be at home, do all the work, because duty had become her habit. She would do whatever he asked her to.

S hrimati looked at the sea with sorrow and bewilderment. The grief that was in her heart was as deep as the ocean. Despite her arguments and her tears he had not listened to her. She sat on a chair and felt as if all her energy had drained out. What had she achieved in her life, she asked herself. She had done everything for Shrikant but he had not noticed her sincerity; he did not value her sacrifices for him.

He had told her that his time was very valuable.

Yes, he would definitely grow in stature and rise to a more prominent position over a period of time. But what about her? She had to live like his shadow all the time. She wouldn't have any identity of her own. Her life would be that of a planet which shines with reflected light, rather than that of a star which radiates its own light.

She also remembered the way he had sneered at her, *The whole world says that you are more intelligent than me. You think over it and whatever you feel is right, go ahead and do it.*

Indeed, what had she really achieved in life? Nothing. A big zero. If they had children, things might have been a bit better. Even if Shrikant spent all his time in office, she could spend her time with the children. But Shrikant had rejected the idea of adoption too. Maybe even if they had children, Shrikant would have sent them to a boarding school like Harish had done. One could never know how Shrikant's mind would work. She thought about her life ten years hence, and shivered. She had always disliked being dependent on anyone.

Living like this was worse than death to her.

Shrimati tried to analyse her feelings. What could make her happy? Her husband's love, and history. Since her husband had made his feelings clear, only history remained. She thought of her college days. Not for a single day was she unhappy. In spite of getting all those gold medals, being offered a scholarship by Professor Collins and the opportunity to go and study abroad, she had rejected them all because she was madly in love with Shrikant. She had voluntarily closed all her career paths. She now felt that her greatest shortcoming was that she was not ambitious. Had she been so, perhaps today she would have become a leading historian of the country . . .

Her mother Kamala's words sprang up in her mind. When the topic of marriage was raised, her mother had said to her that her in-laws would never love her and Shrikant would never treat her better than his people. Is it not true that blood is thicker than water? Shrikant's love had evaporated like water from a cup. Now the cup was empty, and so was her heart. How true had been her mother's prediction!

Shrimati remembered telling Shrikant a few times that his mother always bought the cheapest of gifts for her, but for Rama she would buy things worth thousands! And Shrikant had laughed and said, 'You have more than enough, Shrimati, why should my poor mother give you any gift!'

Shrikant would never understand that a gift is not measured by its price, rather by the feelings behind it. When Gangakka would give her anything, she would purposely keep the price tag on and in front of outsiders she would say, 'Anyway, she is childless and my son is a pot of gold to her. He listens to everything she says and asks for . . .'

Only Shrimati knew how shrewd Shrikant was and how he made people think that he was a *joru ka ghulaam*, a slave of his wife. It was always his decision that prevailed over hers. Why blame others if they believed it? When her husband did not care for her, why would anybody else?

Shrikant's words kept going round and round in Shrimati's head. *You think over it and whatever you feel is right, go ahead and do it.*

Shrikant had never used such words before. She had always thought that Shrikant was proud of her intelligence. So why had he talked like that? Was it to hurt her? If that was so, then why should she remain here? A house is made up of just four walls but a home is where there is love, affection and a meaningful relationship. When that was not there it was only a house, and the best thing was to get out of it. But where could she go? She could not go back to Hubli and make her mother unhappy. The only way for her was to go somewhere she would feel comfortable.

Shrimati had always enjoyed the academic atmosphere and the company of teachers in the University. The only option left was to become a student once again.

Even today, Indian history was at her fingertips. All the facts, dates, events were fresh in her mind. When she read any book on history her concentration was as good as Shrikant's was in computers. She remembered Professor Collins and his last visit. Probably he had made his offer to her because he had sensed her futile existence. Shrimati got up, took a pen and started writing to Professor Collins. She did not mention a word about her personal problems. She stated how studying history had always made her happy . . . The letter exceeded two pages. At the end she wrote, 'Sir, your love for history is not affected by your age. A person like you is always a role model. It would be an honour for me to work under you. The time has come now. I want to do my doctorate. But Sir, without a scholarship, I cannot come. I believe economic independence is one of the most important components of freedom. Kindly let me know your opinion. Please convey my regards to Dorothy.'

By the time she finished, it was long past midnight. Shrimati felt calm and at peace. She slept. The next morning she went and posted the letter herself.

Shrimati's mind had been in turmoil for the last three weeks. At times, she would feel that Professor Collins would arrange a scholarship. But then uncertainty would creep in and she would doubt her own ability. It had been ten years since she had discontinued her studies. Could she catch up and compete with the students who were much younger than her? Would it be possible to concentrate on her studies? Had she taken the decision merely in anger? Was it a proper decision? There were thousands of questions in her mind and she was not able to answer any of them.

Shrikant had called her many times in those three weeks, but her replies had been to the point. When Vasudev Shenoy and his wife visited Bombay, Shrimati duly took care of them as per Shrikant's instructions.

And then one day all her doubts were settled. She got a reply from Professor Collins.

She opened the letter impatiently.

It is quite natural for a scholar like you to wish to become a student again. Getting a scholarship for you is not difficult at all. As there are many things we need to discuss, I feel that you must come at least one week before the term begins. Please do not discard your writings thinking they are outdated. Do bring them. I have asked Dorothy to look for a small apartment for you near the university. Being a vegetarian, it would be better for you to be on your own, than in a dormitory. Until you find something, you can stay in our house. I consider myself lucky to have a student like you at my age. It is rather difficult to have good research students. Dorothy is excited at your arrival. Shrimati, there is no age limit for learning. One who has a thirst for knowledge is a true student. If you have any doubts in your mind about your competence, please forget them.

America is not an unknown country to you. I am sending you the visa papers so that you can come at the earliest.

Shrimati read the letter over and over again. Yes. She could become a student again. She felt life had opened a new door for her. This time, she was making a decision with her head, not with her heart. Sitting in the balcony, she daydreamed about being in a university campus, reading in the library, studying in the classrooms, discussing in the seminar hall. In such places, only knowledge is respected. There is no business talk or pretensions. There is no profit, no loss. How beautiful her life would be! How had she not considered it before, she wondered.

In life, beauty, power, money, health, youth are not constant. Real wealth is knowledge. The more you give, the wealthier you become. That is the reason why teachers are great. Because they spread their knowledge every year to many many students, without expecting any rewards or receiving any favours.

But after the excitement had died down, Shrimati became a little worried. Once she was gone, who would look after Shrikant? Of late, due to continuous tension, his health was not so good. If she wasn't there, it would cause a problem for him. She felt sorry for Shrikant as he had no idea about money or household matters. He would just sign wherever needed. He had so much faith in her that he would not even carry a wallet. If she went away, what would her mother say? What would people say? Would they gossip about their marriage? These conflicting thoughts pulled her in different directions. Her fingers began to pain from gripping the arms of the chair so tightly. Finally, she made up her mind. She could not stay here. She had to go someplace where she could get the same joy that Shrikant got from his work. That pleasure was more valuable than money. She was going away not to earn money, but to find her own individuality.

The story of Bhamati that she had told Shrikant long ago, came back to mind. Every woman could not become Bhamati. Each woman had her own limits and Shrimati too had come to the end of her patience. Was it the difference in their personalities that had made Shrimati take this decision, she wondered. Or was it her unbearable loneliness? She knew that many women go into depression, become alcoholics, and in some cases become kleptomaniacs. Psychiatrists believe that women do this in order to draw the attention of their busy, ambitious husbands.

Shrimati thought of her mother and grandmother. Her grandmother used to say that her grandfather was a terror and did not believe that women were capable of taking decisions. He never gave women any freedom. And yet Rindakka had never spoken ill of him. Her own mother was married to a worthless man, but she still showed him respect and never spoke harsh words to him. Her situation was so different in comparison. Shrikant was unlike either of these two men, but she didn't want to stay on with him.

Her grandmother had never had economic independence so she might have stayed back because of that. Her mother was the sole breadwinner of the family. But she still continued to stay with her husband. That was because they

Sudha Murty

were conditioned to believe that a woman should stay with her husband, irrespective of what he was.

Shrimati did not agree with that belief. She felt that there was a limit to which one could be obedient and subservient, but once that limit was crossed, the individual's happiness became more important.

Shrikant was due to come back the following week. Now that Shrimati had made up her mind, her main concern was how to break the news to him.

Shrikant returned from the hectic four-week business trip. He was extremely tired and slept for a while before going to office. It was impossible for a person like Shrikant to stay at home because of jet lag.

He did not notice anything wrong with Shrimati. He saw that she was cleaning up something, but that was not unusual. Shrimati was extraordinarily neat. He often joked, 'If I don't hold on to the shirt that I am wearing, Shrimati may give it away to somebody while cleaning the cupboard.'

Before leaving for office, he had told Shrimati that he wanted to have an early dinner that day.

Shrimati said, 'Shri, do you have time now? I want to tell you something very urgent.'

'No, Shrimati, I am late already. We will speak over dinner.'

'But, in case you get delayed in coming back from your office, it might be too late.'

'Oh, that's not a problem. I will come early for you today.' He left, not even bothering to ask what the important matter was. He thought it would be one of her impractical ideas.

There was a vast difference between promising something and executing it. But as promised, Shrikant came home early that day. He seemed very excited, jubilant even.

Shrimati was sitting on the sofa, staring at the ceiling. Shrikant did not notice that. He came, threw his coat on the dining table and sat next to her on the sofa. Holding her in his arms he said, 'Hey, Shrimati, today you must congratulate me. I have become the managing director of the company. I have been chosen as one of the top executives of the country. Shrimati, when I was in IIT, my classmates went abroad. But I had said that I would stay in India and achieve more here than they did there. Today I have realized my dream. Now you are the wife of a managing director. Let us move out of this house. We will take up a place in Malabar Hill maybe, overlooking the sea, as per your wish. Shrimati, I do not like to fight with you and I feel extremely unhappy when we quarrel. You should understand that my profession demands all these things. You cannot have the rice and eat it too. Now, I will take some time off. Wherever you want, I will accompany you. I will not go to Hubli. This time, you are my priority.' Like the old days he put his head on her lap and continued to chatter.

Shrimati remained silent.

Whatever he was saying was futile, like pouring water on a stone. Normally, Shrimati would have rejoiced at his promotion, as if it was her own. For the first time she did not feel she was a part of his success. Shrikant found her silence strange and thought she was still angry. He got up and turned her face towards him. He noticed that there were no tears or anger in her eyes. On the contrary, there was a determination and sadness. Shrimati stood up without saying anything.

'Shri, this is the key to the house, and this one to your Godrej almirah. This is the finance file, as of today. Please keep them all carefully.'

Shrikant was puzzled. He did not understand what she was talking about.

'Shrimati, why do I need all these things? Are you going somewhere? Even then I will not need these things.'

Shrimati closed her eyes, used all her willpower and answered slowly.

'Shri, I am leaving and I don't have any plans to return. I am handing over all the responsibilities of the house to you.'

Shrikant was bewildered. 'Where are you going?'

'I am going to the US to do my doctorate. I was just waiting for your return. I have carried out all the instructions that you had given me, completed all the assignments that you had set for me.'

Shrikant's excitement was flattened at once. He just could not comprehend the new situation. He felt as if someone was pushing him from Mount Kailash.

'Shrimati, if you are going to do your Ph.D in the US, then when will you return? How can you take such a major decision without even consulting me? How will you maintain yourself in the US?'

Suddenly Shrikant felt utterly tired and helpless.

'Shri, I am getting a scholarship. I have thought over this matter for the last four weeks before taking this decision. I did not bring anything with me when I got married to you. Now also, I am not taking anything from this house. My flight is scheduled for tonight. I was wondering in case you don't turn up today, how I would perform my last duty. Anyway, you have come and now I can leave peacefully.'

Shrikant's mind had gone numb. Nothing she said was registering. In a disbelieving voice he said, 'Shrimati, are you joking?'

But then his eyes fell on her packed suitcase and he realized it was no joke.

After taking a deep breath, Shrimati continued, 'Shri, you have reached this position today because you are highly focused and you work very very hard. You have dedicated the most important part of your life and all your time to achieving this goal. It is not easy, I agree. Look at your friends who were as bright as you. They have not achieved what you have. You have surpassed everybody in your batch. You started as a software engineer and reached the pinnacle of your career within ten years. In the olden days people used to call this tapasya, penance, and for that they would have to go to the forest. You have achieved it without going to the forest . . .'

Shrikant stopped her, 'But that has nothing to do with your leaving.'

'No, Shri. Listen to me patiently. Very few people can work like you to achieve what you have, not bothering about material benefits or happiness in life. But nothing is free in life, Shri. In achieving your position, you have lost your Shrimati.

'I cannot live in this kind of an atmosphere with these artificial values. I require to breathe fresh air. I do not want to live as your shadow. I want to find my own happiness. Shri, if I had not been sensitive and bright, I wouldn't have had to suffer such loneliness. I could have enjoyed your wealth. When I was thinking about my life so far, what my goal has been, I have realized what I want.'

Shrimati stopped. She was waiting for Shrikant to say something. But he was silent, still in shock.

Shrimati continued.

'Shri, I loved history and I loved you. In fact, once upon a time I loved you more than history. But when you lost your finer sentiments, chasing your success in the world of business, I was left with nothing other than history. For me, the glamour of money, house, car is immaterial. Shri, ask yourself. If you were in my shoes, what would you have done? The same thing that I am doing. Do you remember why you did not take up a job in Hubli? Because you knew your goal. Now, I am also clear about my goal and I want to achieve it. Shri, you are my guru. I learnt this from you. Whenever something new happens, people call it a revolution in the perspective of history and only later appreciate its significance. A running man cannot change his direction all of a sudden. In physics, you call that inertia. I know that if I leave now, it is very natural for society to talk about me. But let me not worry about that. A person can live only by his own faith. He needs to travel on his own path, whether it has stones or thorns. He cannot take some other path, even though it is smooth and rosy, and that is exactly what I am doing today.'

Shrimati talked as if she had never got a chance to speak before. It was like lifting the valve off a pressure cooker. Shrikant just kept looking at Shrimati, his mind completely blank. She continued to speak.

'Shri, what have I done all these years? I used to welcome your guests, keep your accounts, look after the house and fulfil the duties just the way your personal secretary does. I was your valuable, glittering ornament in the social circuit. I no longer want to be that. I want to live the way I want. Shri, I don't want a divorce from you because in my view divorce is merely a document that permits you to remarry. It has no other significance. I do not have any such intentions. You cannot change your lifestyle. You are bound by that. Your job requires that kind of commitment and you cannot live without it. But I cannot adjust to that. In the best interests of both of us, this is the only solution. Shri, you told me the other day that I am more intelligent than you and I can decide what I want. This is what I have decided.'

Shrikant moved for the first time, from his long silence.

Sudha Murty

'Shrimati, don't make an emotional decision. I said so in the heat of anger. Are you aware of the consequences of your decision?'

'Shri, I have thought about everything calmly for the last four weeks. You can definitely live without me. You will find an excellent secretary who can do all this work for you. You may miss me for some time but you will get used to. Shri, if you really need my help, please call me. Wherever I am, I will come and visit you. It is very difficult for me to leave you, but I have no other option. I married you because I loved you. I am not leaving you because of our quarrel. I am not going away because you are angry with me. I am not deserting you either for monetary gain or some other temptation. I am going away only because I want to be like you. You are not like a normal husband who would control his wife . . .'

Shrimati's eyes welled up with tears. She became emotional and there was a catch in her throat. Though she had thought over it and had taken a conscious decision, it was very difficult for her to talk any more. She was scared that if she stayed a little longer she might change her mind and get into the same trap again. She came near Shrikant and said, 'Shri, I am leaving now. My house is always open to you. When you come to the US, do not go away without meeting me. Please keep in touch. Take care of your health. Don't forget to drink skimmed milk. I will not ask you to come and say goodbye. It will be traumatic for both of us. I want to goodbye here itself. Shri, I cannot get a better friend than you.' She kissed his forehead gently, hugged him warmly, then took her small bag and walked out.

She left without even turning back.

Stunned, Shrikant continued to gaze at her back. He felt that she was taking his spirit away with her.

The click of the door told Shrikant that Shrimati had gone. But he just could not believe that such a thing had happened. The Shrimati he saw that day was so different from the Shrimati he thought he knew. What she was and what he had thought about her was entirely contradictory. He had thought that she did not have the strength to withstand social stigma and lacked great will power.

Shrikant was caught in a whirlpool of thoughts. Why did Shrimati do this? As far as he remembered her from their childhood days, she was shy but different from most women. She was bright and, most important, she was obedient. And that could be the reason that he had ignored her, because she was not aggressive and demanding. While other men in the office would say that they had to go home early and they could not work on Sundays, he used to make fun of them, 'Oh, you do not know how to tell your wife. Look at me. My wife will never question me.' He remembered that once Harish told him, 'Shrikant, neither you nor your wife are normal. You are a lucky man. You do not have any family problem.'

But now, he could understand what it had meant.

When his chairman called him personally to congratulate him after his promotion, he was very proud of his success. He thought all his success was due to his own efforts. Now he thought of Shrimati. What was her share in his achievement? She always wished him progress, silently and constantly suffered her loneliness. Actually she had deserved a lion's share in his achievements. But he never acknowledged it. Today, she had broken his pride by rejecting his position, his achievements and leaving him.

Shrikant was amazed to see the papers that Shrimati had left for him. Why did Shrimati leave him? She had said she wanted clean air. Was this atmosphere suffocating her? In any business party, looking at profit and loss is a corporate culture. It is not philanthropy or history. Why did Shrimati take it personally? Was Shrimati scaring him? Had she gone for a few days? Though his heart wanted it to be that way, his mind said that it was not true.

He thought once again. No one in this male-dominated society would appreciate her step but Shrimati had left him without even bothering about what people would think. She had acted on what she felt was right. Many more thoughts were constantly breaking like waves in his mind. Was it his mother who used to deliberately insult her and his sister who would taunt her that had made Shrimati bitter? It might have been one of the reasons for her decision. He felt guilty about it for the first time. He compared Shrimati's difficulties with Rama's, forgetting their level of sensitivity. Rama was so insensitive that she could quarrel with anybody and still go to that person's house for dinner. How had he never thought about it?

His memory went back to the story of Bhamati, the woman who had dedicated her entire life to her husband and he felt Shrimati was a shade better than Bhamati, who had never seen the outside world and did not know her capacity. Shrimati had served her husband with single-minded devotion knowing her capabilities and being aware of the outside world.

Her husband recognized his wife's sacrifice and named the book after her. That is what appeals to me more. Shrikant recollected what Shrimati had said long back.

But, in her real life, her husband did not even recognize her sacrifice! How cruel it was for Shrimati . . .

Shrikant felt pained. 'Oh, Shrimati, I cannot live without you. You are my source of energy and inspiration. I can see the influence of your personality in all my work. Without you, I am incomplete.' But he knew that it was too late. There were many pictures that came to his mind.

When they had had less money, she would always save enough for him to buy books. Even though they were newly married, she wouldn't disturb him while he was reading at home; rather, in their small house, she would sit in the kitchen and read some books. He remembered now how much she used to go out of her way to please his mother. In return, what did she get? Sheer rejection from his family and his negligence.

Our myths say that during the churning of the oceans, the dangerous poison haalahala came out, but there was no taker for that. Then, Lord Shiva drank it for the benefit of mankind . . .

Poor Shrimati swallowed every poisonous insult, just to keep Shrikant happy.

Probably, children would have been the link that would have held their marriage together. But he might have kept them in a boarding school, like his colleagues had done, and pushed Shrimati to further sorrow. He was a man who could not take 'a negative answer' for anything. Be it any matter, it was his decision that was final. He wanted to win in every situation. He was a headstrong person and it was a wonder how she had coped with him.

The cool breeze from the balcony blew into the hall and the keys on the table fell down. The papers flew in different directions. Shrikant did not have the energy to get up and collect them. He was worried about how she would live in the US without much money. She did not have any expensive habits though. If she had, she would not have left him. He was amazed at her meticulous entries of all the accounts. When he looked at the different keys, he did not know which was what. Everything was hurting him now. He had treated her just like an assistant and she had told him that he could get a better one. Was it ever possible? Nobody would do this kind of work for money. Shrimati had done it out of sheer love for Shrikant.

Shrikant could hear the sound of the rain. It was Shravan, the rainy season, and it was pouring cats and dogs in Bombay. He returned to the real world. He was a man of action. Whatever had happened had happened. He felt he had to set things right. He had to tell his mother to love Shrimati. Then he realized what a futile exercise that would be. People cannot be taught or told to love; it should arise on its own.

Where was Shrimati now? Had she reached the international airport? He felt like going and bringing her back. But his enthusiasm disappeared like a bubble when he thought about it rationally. If he brought Shrimati home, could he be the same Shrikant he was ten years ago? That was impossible. Shrikant was incapable of living the kind of life Shrimati wanted. He had lost the ability to love anyone selflessly or to open up to anybody because the world of business had changed him deeply. He had reached such a height that he could not come down. Even if Shrimati had stayed in Bombay and done her doctorate she wouldn't be happy as he would not be able to change his ways.

She was educated, knowledgeable and good-natured. He had used her for his advantage. That was the reason Shrimati had gone away. All these thoughts revealed themselves to Shrikant, layer by layer.

He became extremely angry with himself. He felt helpless. He was a victim of power, ambition, status and success.

The sea was roaring as if it had witnessed the terrible tragedy. Suddenly, Shrikant remembered Ravi's letter. *When I think of Shrimati, I continue to be amazed by her clear thinking and her wise decisions, like when she chose to join arts college in spite of getting the first rank in her tenth board exams. Do you remember that we had laughed at her? Now when I look back, I feel she was the brightest. She knew what she liked and she did exactly that. Shrikant, you are very lucky to get such a companion.*

He regretted his actions now, after losing the fortune he had forgotten he possessed. He experienced the same shock, the same disappointment and the same agony that he had felt when he had lost his first rank, seventeen years ago. After all these years Shrikant felt that he had then lost a meaningless rank, but today, he had lost his most precious Shrimati.

What would Shrimati be doing now, he wondered, looking at his watch. Maybe the mandatory custom checking is over. His eyes were full of tears, realizing that there would be nobody to even say goodbye to her. She was all alone. *What would their mothers think?* But it did not matter what people thought. What was important was that Shrimati had made her decision.

He always thought that his own life was much more significant than hers and his own will stronger. But now he stood disheartened without Shrimati.

Sudha Murty

The telephone rang, waking Shrikant up from his thoughts. The sound of the roaring sea and the pouring rain was ringing in his ears.

It was Harish. 'Shrikant, congratulations. It seems our road show has been cleared. If all of us participate in that, then probably we may be listed in the New York Stock Exchange. It is all because of your hard work . . .' Sensing the silence that was unusual, Harish continued, 'Shrikant, can you hear me?'

'Yes, I can. But . . .'

'There is no but for you, Shrikant. You are the leader of leaders. Without you, the road show will not take place.'

Shrikant felt the old excitement flood through him. 'Hey, Harish. I will come to office right now.'

'At this odd hour?'

'For success there is no odd and even hours. Every minute is precious. I will go to office and work on that. I want the list of the places that we are going to visit, the budget and other details. I have been thinking about the premium on the share issue . . .' Shrikant went on.

As he talked, he heard a plane flying over Bandra, and he forgot what he was saying. The receiver was in his hand but he was looking at the sky. He saw the red tail lamp of a plane in the dark sky.

Shrimati, who had walked with him side by side in the same Shravan rain for ten years had now left him all alone.